Praise for Ann Charles

Don't Let It Snow In Deadwood

"Ann Charles sucked me in with characters I want to spend the holidays with! Laced with humor, friendship, a really good man, a runaway chicken, misplaced mistletoe, and lots of family drama to sweeten the tea, there is nothing cold about this book except the snow. It gave me all the feels!"
~Renee George, USA Today Bestselling Author of the Peculiar Mystery Series

"*Don't Let It Snow In Deadwood* comes complete with a wild blizzard, plenty of Christmas spirit, and a dysfunctional family gathering that delivers more than one holiday surprise. A real Christmas treat for fans old and new of the Deadwood Mystery Series!"
~Joleen James, Award-winning Author of the Hometown Alaska Men Series and Wilding Point Romance Series

"Grab a cup of eggnog and curl up with the gang as they celebrate Christmas—Deadwood-style. Will Violet Parker end up on the naughty list? This must-read addition to Ann's series will leave you warm and fuzzy and howling with laughter!"
~Kristy McCaffrey, Author of the Award-winning Wings of the West Series

"Witty, joyful, and full of surprises! Wouldn't expect anything less!"
~Rebecca Lyndsey, Author of the Children's Book, *Into the Ocean*

Dear Reader,

When I started writing this book, I planned to give you a glimpse of Violet's family holiday with some of the usual Christmas traditions thrown into the mix. I had a short tale in mind, nothing more than a few chapters' worth of laughs, but I should've known better. As soon as Violet stepped onto the scene in Chapter One, she scoffed at the idea of a short story, grabbed my hand, and took off running. Nineteen chapters later, the tenth book in the Deadwood Mystery Series was born.

To celebrate this milestone in the series, DON'T LET IT SNOW IN DEADWOOD offers a little something new:

It's a story about family.

It's a story about snow.

It's a story about the roller-coaster emotions and head-banging frustrations that come with too much family and snow. Full of twists and turns, and a jaw-dropper or two, this triple-sized holiday tale should last longer than a double decaf low-fat latte with medium foam dusted with a breath of nutmeg and a tiny sprinkle of crushed candy canes.

We're ten books into the Deadwood Mystery Series now. A lot has happened so far, changing Violet's life in ways she never imagined. We've laughed, cringed, flinched, snorted, sighed, guffawed, cursed, and cheered along with Violet and her friends. Raise your glass and let's toast to even wilder times yet to come.

I leave you with one of Old Man Harvey's favorite quotes:

"Learn this well, the last ride is never the last ride. And the end is not the end." ~ Richard A. Rowland

Enjoy the snowy ride!

Ann Charles

www.anncharles.com

DEADWOOD
MYSTERY SERIES

DON'T LET IT SNOW IN DEADWOOD

Book 10

ANN CHARLES

Illustrated by C.S.Kunkle

For Diane Garland
*(aka the brainiac who helps me keep track of the story world details for my Deadwood
Mystery Series, as well as all of my other books and series)*

*Thanks for locking me in your basement and making me write a
holiday story that is three times longer than I'd planned. Next time
can I have more sugar in my gruel? Pretty please?*

You are awesome, my wonderfully nit-picky friend!

Cover Art by C.S. Kunkle
Cover Design by B Biddles
Editing by Eilis Flynn
Formatting by B Biddles

Library of Congress 2018911980
E-book ISBN-13: 978-1-940364-57-5
Print ISBN-13: 978-1-940364-58-2

Acknowledgments

This book had a lot of help from so many elves. Thanks to:

My husband, the head-honcho elf, for your help with brainstorming, editing, formatting, designing the cover, and keeping the kids and me fat and happy.

My kids, the cookie-eating elves, for always being so willing to share celebratory frozen Cokes with me.

My first-draft elves: Margo Taylor, Mary Ida Kunkle, Kristy McCaffrey, Jacquie Rogers, Marcia Britton, Paul Franklin, Diane Garland, Vicki Huskey, Lucinda Nelson, Marguerite Phipps, Stephanie Kunkle, and Wendy Gildersleeve. Your patience rivals that of a Jedi master some weeks.

My critique-buddy elves, Jacquie Rogers and Kristy McCaffrey, for maintaining your top spots on the Naughty List.

My editor elf, Eilis Flynn, for helping to make the words on the page sparkle and shine brighter (and wearing awesome socks).

My story-keeper elf, Diane Garland, for stuffing my stocking with chocolate-covered coffee beans.

My beta-team elves for celebrating the holiday months ahead of time with me and checking my book for burned-out bulbs.

My artsy elf, C.S. Kunkle, for moving to Arizona so we could work on cover art and illustrations by your pool during the snowy season.

All of you reader elves for your encouraging emails and social media posts AND for your face-to-face smiles and hugs. Without you by my side, this would be a long, lonely sleigh ride through the snow.

Kickbutt-author elf Renee George for your nutcrackin' cover quote and funny movie reviews!

And as always, a special thanks to Clint-the-clown elf for keeping me company on that crazy bus trip back to Ohio many moons ago. If we had to do it again, I'd let you get the large fries this time.

Also by Ann Charles

Cast

KEY: Character (Book # in which they appear)—Description****

Violet Lynn Parker (1–10)—Heroine of the series, real estate agent

Willis "Old Man" Harvey (1–10)—Violet's sidekick and so-called bodyguard

Dane "Doc" Nyce (1–10)—Violet's boyfriend, medium

Detective "Coop" Cooper (1–10)—Deadwood and Lead's detective

Zoe Parker (1–10)—Violet's aunt and mentor in life

Layne Parker (1–10)—Violet's nine-year-old son

Adelynn Parker (1–10)—Violet's nine-year-old daughter

Natalie Beals (1–10)—Violet's best friend since childhood

Cornelius Curion (3–10)—Violet's client; so-called ghost-whisperer

Reid Martin (2–10)—Captain of the fire dept., Aunt Zoe's ex-lover

Susan Parker (1–10)—Violet's evil sister; aka "the Bitch from Hell"

Quint Parker (1–3,7–10)—Violet's brother; Layne's hero

Blake Parker (8,10)—Violet's father

Hope Parker (1-2,8,10)—Violet's mother

Freesia Tender (5–10)—Owner of the Galena House

Rex Conner (3–8,10)—Biological father of Violet's children

Jane Grimes (1–10)—Violet's previous boss

Dominick Masterson (4,7–10)—Previous client of Violet's old boss, Jane.

"When things go wrong, don't go with them." ~Elvis Presley

Chapter One

The Black Hills, South Dakota
Christmas Eve
7:36 p.m.

Winter wonderland, my ass," I bellyached, my teeth chattering while the frigid wind rocked me in my boots. Snow pelted my face, sticking to my eyelashes.

I shivered, my shoulders pulling in tight as I stood in the middle of the two-lane highway. My SUV's headlights blazed from behind me, but in a storm this fierce, the bright beams of light weren't much help. They reflected off the swirling flakes, blinding me rather than illuminating the vast stretch of dark, empty snow-covered road in front of me.

Old Man Winter could be such a dick. He'd gone and coated the hills in a thick blanket of white on Christmas Eve of all days. It was going to take at least a week of December sunshine to melt this white fluffy crap away. I scowled long and hard, not giving a flying reindeer if my face froze that way either.

The wind raged and howled around me, tearing through

my blue wool coat. It stole my breath and gripped my bones with its freezing fingers. I tucked my scarf tighter around me, weighing my options. The blizzard had crowded into the Black Hills so fast, pushing and shoving to make it in time for Christmas.

Trudging ahead through the frozen tundra would be right up there with dodging icebergs in the North Atlantic. Besides, my new purple snow boots were no match for the drifts, many of which were already knee-deep and rising.

"Razzle-frazzit," I muttered through stiff lips.

Down on the prairie in the warm bosom of my parents' house, my two kids were waiting for Santa and me to show. Earlier on the phone, I'd reassured them the snowy roads wouldn't stop me from arriving in time to help them prep for St. Nick. Little had I realized then that Old Man Winter had a plan to knock me on my caboose and then kick me while I was down.

But I wasn't waving any white flags yet. Nope. I still had plenty of grit in my gizzard. Raising my gloved hands, I aimed both middle fingers at the sky. "Kiss off, icehole!"

A strong gust of wind rammed me from behind, knocking me to my hands and knees in the snow. Cold wetness soaked through my jeans and gloves. Before I could catch my breath, another blast of air hit me, blowing snow into my face.

Son of a sugarplum!

I wiped at my eyes with my coat sleeve. Rolling onto my back, I stared up at the maelstrom whirling overhead. Somehow, I had to make it to my kids through this frozen wasteland.

Chapter Two

Six Hours Earlier …

The only way I could think to keep this Christmas from ending in disaster was to poison my sister.

As I killed the lights in Calamity Jane Realty's office, my cell phone rang. A glance at the screen made me curse. Unfortunately, my mother was one step ahead of me, doing her damnedest to interfere with my sister's untimely demise.

Buttoning my wool coat, I accepted the call. "What now, Mom?"

"Really, Violet Lynn?" my mother scolded. "You're going to take that tone with me on Christmas Eve?"

"You've called me like five times in the last two hours."

Something thumped overhead. I frowned at the ceiling. What was that? Other than me, myself, and I, the building was supposed to be empty. My coworkers and boss hadn't even come into work today, and our upstairs neighbor was out of town.

"If you were down here already as we'd planned," Mom's voice interrupted my what-the-hell moment, "I wouldn't have to keep calling you."

As we'd planned? I gritted my molars. Was she smoking mistletoe leaves? Until yesterday morning, *my plan* was to enjoy Christmas Eve here in Deadwood with my kids, Aunt Zoe, and Doc, my boyfriend. Then, on Christmas afternoon, we'd drive down to my parents' place for a family dinner. That was all. The end.

But yesterday morning, everything had changed when the TV weather guy started squawking about the sky falling and burying the hills up to their cockles in a shitload of snow. Of course, that made my mom freak out in true Chicken Little style, calling me in a panic to rant that she'd filled the refrigerator and deep freezer with hundreds of dollars' worth of food and piled presents under her tree, all for us. In other words, if the kids, Doc, and I were stuck in Deadwood because of a blizzard, Christmas would surely end in a tragedy that rivaled Shakespeare's *Macbeth*.

Suddenly, my cozy Christmas Eve fantasy filled with visions of snuggling in front of the blinking tree lights with a plate of sugar cookies and a mug of hot buttered rum had disappeared in a puff of chimney smoke. The next thing I knew, Mom had beseeched and bribed Aunt Zoe to haul Addy and Layne down yesterday to spend the night with her and my dad, leaving Doc and me to follow when I finished with work today.

What was supposed to be a three-hour family Christmas dinner event had morphed. Now I was looking at a hellish two-night stay—maybe even three if the blizzard hung around to pester western South Dakota as long as the local meteorologists were forecasting.

It was because of this change in plans that I was wondering where I could buy a vial of poison on Christmas Eve for my sister, Susan, whom I'd lovingly nicknamed "The Bitch from Hell" many moons ago.

Susan had moved back home semi-recently, setting up her fiery lair in my parents' basement. Susan's modus operandi since childhood had been to seek and destroy anything special to me, including my relationships with various men over the years. It wasn't enough for her that she'd popped out of our mother's womb having everything I didn't—long legs, a model-thin body, straight brunette hair, and a black soul overflowing with mischief. Okay, so maybe we shared that last trait along with matching heart-shaped lips.

My point, which I spelled out in loud enunciated words to my mom yesterday, was that it'd be impossible for my sister and me to endure each other's company for forty-eight hours without something getting broken, such as Susan's neck, followed of course by my mother's heart. Breaking my mom's heart would land me in a heap of trouble with my father, whom I adored to pieces. Therein lay the main setback to my poisoning plot.

Snapping back to the present task of making it out of Deadwood before the snow hit, I took a calming breath and returned to my conversation with my mom. "As I told you five phone calls ago, I couldn't come down yesterday because I had to show a couple of houses this morning." I opened the office's back door, hunching into my coat at the blast of cold air that greeted me.

She scoffed through the phone. "Who goes house shopping on Christmas Eve?"

"Potential buyers who are in town visiting family for the holidays, that's who." I locked the door and scurried across the parking lot toward my Honda SUV. "This was the only day that worked for both of our schedules, so I had to stay in Deadwood."

"Well, I think it's selfish of them to make you work on Christmas Eve."

"So you've said over and over and over and—"

"You know, if you manage not to screw up things with your boyfriend this time and actually snag a wedding ring in the deal, you could probably quit that job of yours and focus on being a good little homemaker."

I pulled my phone away and scowled at it before holding it back to my ear. "There are so many things wrong with what you just said, Mother. You seem to be forgetting about the fact that Susan stole a couple of potential husbands away from me."

She pshawed through the line. "Those boys weren't

marriage worthy and you know it. You really need to try to focus on the positive."

"Positive, right. Help me out here. What could be positive about walking in on my sister screwing my boyfriend in my own bed?"

She sighed, as if I were the one being melodramatic today. "Try to think of it as Susan saved you from years of anger and frustration, possibly even divorce."

My gaze narrowed, red clouding the outer edges of my vision. "Mom, has Susan been slipping drops of LSD into your morning coffee?"

"Don't be silly, Violet. All I'm saying is that you've been working hard to provide for your family ever since the twins were born. Your doctor fellow is a good egg. Don't break him."

She'd met Doc once while she was drunk, and already he rated higher in her esteem than I did. "His *name* is 'Doc,' Mom, which is short for 'D' and 'R,' his first two initials. He's not an actual doctor, you know."

"Of course, but doctor or not, he knows how to hold onto his money. That's a skill you could stand to learn with the way dollar bills have always slipped through your fingers."

I kicked my back tire. Twice.

What dollar bills? Hell, I'd been scraping by on spare change for the last decade. "Was there a purpose for this call, Mother?" Something besides reminding me of my shortcomings when it came to my finances, along with my multiple calamities with the opposite sex?

"Yes. Addy wants you to bring Buck when you come down this afternoon."

Buck was my daughter's stuffed white unicorn with a pink horn that she cuddled with most nights. "She slept without Buck last night. Why does she need him now?"

"She insists Christmas will be miserable without him."

I rolled my eyes. I translated that to mean Addy would make *my* Christmas miserable if I didn't take her that dang unicorn. "Fine, I'll grab Buck. Anything else?"

A snowflake drifted down in front of me.

Then another.

Then several more.

"She also wants you to bring the game Twister."

"Who's going to want to play that game after stuffing ourselves to the gills with meat and pie? If I bend over, something will probably come back up the pipe."

"Really, Violet? That's disgusting."

Maybe so, but it was the truth. "What's wrong with the games you have there?"

"We don't have Twister."

"Fine, Twister and Buck." I crawled inside my SUV and closed the door. "Anything else?"

"Did I just hear a car door shut?"

"Yes, I'm leaving work and going home to grab the bag of gifts from Santa."

Plus I needed to make sure Addy's cat, gerbil, and chicken were taken care of with food and water for the night. My self-appointed bodyguard, Old Man Harvey, would be stopping by at some point each day while we were down with my parents to check on Addy's pets until we returned home.

"Good. Then you'll be on your way down here soon. Your father is looking forward to visiting with your handsome doctor."

I didn't even bother wasting breath on correcting her again. Knowing my father, "interrogating" was a more fitting description of how their conversations would go. Doc was the first man I'd brought home since my son was born, and Layne didn't really count since he was related to my father by blood and couldn't really talk for the first year of questioning.

"I have to swing by Natalie's place before we leave," I told Mom.

My best friend was staying in Deadwood this holiday instead of spending it with her parents, who were traveling to see Natalie's younger brother. She planned to hang out with her landlady in the Galena House, an old boarding house located one block up from Deadwood's Main Street.

"What? Why?" Mom asked.

"Nat and I haven't had a chance to exchange gifts yet. It will only take a few minutes."

"Sweetheart, you're running out of time!"

I was running out of patience with my dear mother, too. Honestly, what was the rush to put Susan and me in the ring together? Did my parents have a bet going on who'd score the first piledriver?

"Mom, it only takes forty-five minutes to get to your house."

"Sure, if the roads are clear and dry. Haven't you been watching the forecast?"

I stuck the keys in the ignition. "I thought we'd established that I was working this morning."

"The news channels are all calling for a terrible blizzard."

"The news channels are exaggerating." I started my engine, shivering in the cold air blowing out the vents. "They're trying to scare people into staying off the roads. Besides, you know my theory."

"Violet Lynn, don't be absurd. The local weather folks do not consult a Magic 8 ball to determine the forecast. They use computers now instead." The sound of glass breaking came through the line, followed by my dad shouting, "Layne, get the broom!"

I cringed, hoping my kids hadn't broken anything I'd need to apologize for with dollars as well as words. "Listen, Mom, I need to go so we get there before dark, and you need to clean up whatever just broke."

"Be careful, dear. It's getting scary outside."

Who was she kidding? Satan's concubine and I were going to be spending the holiday together under one roof. It was going to be absolutely terrifying *inside* before long, too.

Chapter Three

My mother, loving flower child that she was, didn't understand the depths of Susan's depravity. Hell, the *Titanic* hadn't sunk as deep as that bitch. She didn't just kick ass and take names. Oh no, Susan always made sure to shoot the wounded, too.

Five minutes after I hung up with my love-blinded mom, I pulled into Aunt Zoe's driveway. Inside, I grabbed the garbage bag full of Santa's gifts for the kids and set it by the front door. Another smaller bag with other gifts, including Natalie's, was already in the back seat of my SUV.

I took the stairs two at a time, swinging by my bedroom to change into jeans and a sweater before heading to my daughter's room. I filled one bowl with cat food and two with water for Bogart, Addy's vegetarian cat, who preferred to hide in her closet when not gifting me with living critters in my bed. A check on Duke the gerbil found him working out on his wheel with plenty of pellets and hay in his cage along with a full water bottle. I stood for a moment, watching him make the wheel spin. I should take a lesson from the rodent after all of the Christmas goodies I'd been gorging on lately. Shaking out of my daze, I grabbed Twister and Buck the unicorn before I headed downstairs.

A few minutes later, down in the basement, Elvis the chicken clucked at me from her roost inside her cage. I added a bit more feed to her bowl and wished her a Merry Christmas, leaving the basement light on so she didn't have to spend the holiday in the dark.

That dang chicken was starting to make me soft.

After turning the thermostat down a few notches, I

pulled on my blue wool coat and placed the overnight tote of clothes that I'd packed last night next to the bag of Santa's gifts. Next came Doc's gifts from where I'd hidden them in the bottom of Aunt Zoe's china hutch.

I frowned unseeingly toward the kitchen, worrying about my gifts for Doc. This was the first Christmas with a man in my life other than my father, son, and brother. Choosing the perfect gift had inspired a lot of knuckle chewing, so I'd picked out several possibilities with the hope that I'd hit somewhere close to the bull's-eye with one of them.

My cell phone rang as I grabbed my stocking hat and gloves from the dining room table.

"Not again, Mom," I grumbled, fishing my phone from my pocket.

It wasn't my mom. My heart pitter-pattered. "*Bonjour, mon cher*," I purred.

"Ah, Tish, that's French." Doc's deep voice warmed me through the line. "Hurry up and get over here so I can kiss my way up your arm," he flirted, playing along in our Gomez and Morticia Addams game.

"You miss me already?" I teased.

He and I had the house to ourselves last night since Aunt Zoe and the kids were down in Rapid City. The fooling around had started on the couch after I crawled on his lap, flashed my bare sugarplums at him, and showed him exactly what I wanted for Christmas. We moved to the floor several moans and groans later where I worked my magic heating up his Yule log. The tree lights added a colorful glow to Doc's skin as I kissed every inch of him, doing my darnedest to spread Christmas joy throughout his land.

"I miss your lips," he said in a husky voice. "And your sugarplums."

All of a sudden my wool coat felt like a goose-down

parka made to withstand Antarctic winters. I fanned my collar. "Be careful, big boy. If you keep talking dirty to me, you'll end up on the Naughty list."

"Me? What about you?"

I faked a haughty scoff. "I'm a good girl."

He chuckled. "That game you played with me and that red ribbon was very naughty."

"A peppermint stick is meant to be licked. I was merely following proper etiquette." I unplugged the Christmas lights in the living room, smiling down at the floor where I'd worked him into a lather while demonstrating exactly how one savored a peppermint stick.

"Your demonstrations of proper etiquette are going to be the death of me, woman."

"What can I say? I enjoy jingling your bells." I slipped the straps of my overnight tote over my shoulder. "I'm about to head out the door at Aunt Zoe's. Do you need anything from here?"

"Just a sexy blonde with killer curves."

"It's your lucky day, then. One blonde coming up."

"Good. Get those sweet lips over here. The snow is really starting to come down."

I peeked out the window next to the door. The snowflakes were falling with purpose now. "I made sure the tire chains are in the back of my rig."

"Keep your fingers crossed we don't need them."

"I need to swing by Nat's apartment to drop off her gift, then I'll be there to grab you." I snickered. "When I'm done having my wicked way with you, we can hit the road."

"That's it, Boots. No more spiked eggnog for you."

Au contraire, mon cher. I had a feeling I was going to need to keep hitting the hard liquor hourly to get through the next two days without tackling Susan and rubbing gum in her hair. Her history of stealing my boyfriends had me wanting to lock Doc away in a sarcophagus and feed him red and green Jell-O via a straw through a hole in the lid.

"Why isn't Natalie coming with us?" Doc asked.

"She's going to hang out with Freesia tomorrow. Nat doesn't want to leave her alone."

Freesia was Natalie's landlady. Her parents had moved to Nevada, leaving Freesia the boarding house, her family's legacy. But the Galena House had turned into more work than Freesia could handle and afford, so she'd traded free rent in exchange for Natalie's handywoman help fixing up the place to sell.

"You'd better make your visit brief," Doc said. "We don't want to get caught in this storm. The forecast is calling for up to three feet of snow by tomorrow morning in some areas of the hills."

"I'll believe it when I see it."

"Doubt away, sweetheart, but there's a Colorado low front that has formed on the eastern slope of the Rockies, and it's flowing north right into that frigid air blast coming down from Alberta. That's a guaranteed recipe for major snow."

I paused with my hand on the doorknob. "Are you moonlighting as a meteorologist in between planning what people should do with their money?"

He chuckled. "Growing up in the Rockies where blizzards hit in the blink of an eye turned me into a bit of a weather geek."

I opened the door. The snow was falling even faster than moments ago. Crud. There'd be no living with my mother if this truly were a blizzard. "I'll hurry with Natalie."

"Harvey's making cookies for us to take down to your parents," Doc said as I shut the door behind me.

"What's he doing home? I thought he was going to his sister's with Cooper this morning."

Besides being Detective Cooper's uncle, Harvey and the Deadwood detective shared a streak of orneriness and a love of guns. Both had turned down my invitation to join us at Aunt Zoe's Christmas Eve back before our plans had changed thanks to this stupid snowstorm.

"Cooper's still at work, and Harvey doesn't want to get stuck at his sister's due to the blizzard, so he's staying here. He said something about a movie marathon on the Old West channel."

Harvey and Cooper were both living at Doc's place while I tried to sell the former's ranch and help the latter buy a new house.

"He's staying home on Christmas?" The idea of Harvey all alone knotted up my heartstrings.

"I invited him to join us, but he says he has a duty to watch Addy's pets and turned me down."

Addy's pets could go a few days on their own—well, maybe not the chicken.

I hefted the bag of Santa's presents. "I'll deal with Harvey when I get to your place."

"Okay. Call me when you're leaving Natalie's."

"Will do. See you soon, Candy Cane."

Doc groaned at my new pet name for him and hung up.

I loaded the presents and my overnight tote into my Honda and rolled down the street toward Natalie's place. The side streets were coated in white but not slippery yet.

Natalie was coming down the stairs when I rushed inside the boarding house. Her smile was big—a little too big. Her eyes dipped at the edges, a sad glint in their depths. One strap of her green overalls was unlatched, her red sweater only half-tucked.

"Merry almost Christmas," she said, sitting down a few steps from the bottom. She patted the step next to her.

"Merry Christmas back at ya." I dropped next to her, holding out her Christmas gift.

She smelled like a tropical drink, something with pineapple. Her brown hair was damp and hanging loose around her shoulders, curling slightly at the ends. She must be fresh from the shower.

"You okay, Nat?"

"Yeah, sure, why wouldn't I be?" She sounded cheery enough, but she didn't meet my eyes.

I had an idea what was haunting her, and it wasn't any of the boarding house's ghosts. It was more of a case of *who*, and he was very much alive and a major pain in the ass for both Natalie and me.

"Cooper didn't stop by, did he?"

Her cheeks darkened, her gaze still averted. "Of course not. Why would he?"

Uh, maybe because he was one hundred percent nutcrackers over Natalie. Unfortunately for Cooper, Natalie was on sabbatical from men in an effort to rebuild her self-esteem and patch up her heart after multiple attempts to blast both to smithereens.

"I don't know," I lied. "Doc said he's still at work, so I thought he might be doing rounds or something."

She scowled at me. "Your nose is twitching."

I covered my tattletale appendage. "It's itchy."

"And now your pants are on fire." She shook her head. "You really need to learn how to lie without twitching like a mouse or Susan the snake is going to swallow you whole."

Natalie knew all about my sister's forked tongue. She'd grown up with me, stepping in to fight my battles for me when I was too worn down to stand on my own.

She shook the present I'd given her. "It's heavy. Don't tell me you bought me another Ming vase?"

"Nothing but the best for you, girlfriend."

"Ahh, you're the best-est bestie around." She tore off the paper and opened the box. "Holy holly berries! Where did you find a pink hammer?"

"None of your beeswax. Look at the inscription." I pointed at the words etched into the hammer's head.

" 'To Natalie, 'til death do us part. Love, Vi,' " she read aloud. "Creepy and sweet, just like your love." She grinned, gripping it in her right hand. "So, do I get to use this to knock some sense into you the next time you try to ditch me for a man?"

"In a heartbeat."

She looped her arm around my shoulders and hugged me, and then handed me a gift the size of a shoebox.

It was sort of heavy. I shook it. Something metal sounding clanked inside. "Is it bars of gold?"

"Even better."

I ripped off the paper and sliced through the tape with my car keys. Inside the box were two small chrome discs with jaguars etched into them and three prongs sticking out from around the center hubs.

"Is this the newest trend in friendship charms?"

She picked one up from the box. "They're a little too heavy to wear around our wrists, but we could hang them from our rearview mirrors. However, since they're the wheel knockoffs from your ex's fancy-schmancy Jaguar, you might want to keep them hidden from a certain Deadwood detective for a few months."

My ex, Rex Conner, aka the piece-of-shit sperm donor, had recently returned to the Black Hills to mess with my life for shits and giggles. He denied his return was meant to thwart me, insisting he merely wanted to use me and my children for a career advancement. The dickhead was leading a team of scientists at the research lab in Lead down in what used to be the one and only vast Homestake Gold Mine.

"What are wheel knockoffs?"

"The decorative covers for the lug nuts."

"Rex's wheels aren't going to fall off without these, right?" As much as I loathed the man and wanted to have him relocated to one of Saturn's moons, I didn't want to be responsible for his death. At least not at Christmastime. Valentine's Day might be more appropriate for the big jerk.

"Unfortunately, no," Natalie said.

"That's too bad. Are these expensive?"

"They're only about fifty bucks, but on the annoyance scale, I think this will make Rex's sphincter squeeze up good and tight."

A Christmas present centered around revenge. Natalie knew my hopes and dreams so well. I giggled with a good dose of evil and hugged her. "You're the best friend ever."

"Takes one to know one."

Speaking of friends, I glanced up the stairs. "Where's Freesia?"

Natalie set the wheel knockoffs back in the shoebox. "She went to Nevada."

"What?" I frowned at her. "I thought you were going to spend Christmas watching Bogart movies and pigging out on pie together."

"Her dad hasn't been feeling well lately. When she heard about the snowstorm, she decided to head out before she got stuck here and help her mom take care of him."

"So you're coming with Doc and me." It wasn't a question.

"Nah. I'll just stay here and keep fixing up the place." She held up the hammer. "And now I have a new tool to help me."

"No, you won't." I stood, pointing up the stairs. "Go pack a couple of nights' worth of clothes."

She clasped her hands between her knees. "Vi, this Christmas is about Doc spending time with you and your family."

"I know. You're part of my family, fruitcake. Besides, Doc will insist we come get you when he hears you're going to be alone, and we don't have a lot of time with this storm moving in, so go get your shit and let's haul ass."

"But …" She hesitated.

I reached down and pulled her up by the elbow. "The kids and my parents will love having you there, too."

"I don't—"

"*And* I'll need your help terrorizing the Wicked Witch of the West." Natalie had long ago made it her mission in life to fuck with Susan's mental well-being every chance she could as payback for the tramp's many crimes against my heart. "You don't want to miss this special holiday opportunity, do you?"

She cocked one eyebrow. "So Susan is definitely going to be there?" At my nod, she smiled banana-wide. Her eyes sparkled with mischief, her blues long gone. "Well, then let's go have us some rootin'-tootin' Christmas fun."

Chapter Four

Do you remember that Christmas when Santa brought you one of those kid ovens and you made your brother and me itsy-bitsy amoeba-shaped buttons to eat?" Natalie asked as she loaded her duffel bag into the back seat of my SUV.

"Yeah, I was like nine and those were supposed to be miniature chocolate chip cookies, thank you very much." I slid behind the steering wheel, blinking the snowflakes from my eyelashes.

That might have been the last time I tried my hand at baking. Like rocket science and quantum physics, cooking was one of those highly technical skills that eluded me. It was a major accomplishment most days when I could make a bowl of cereal without somehow burning it.

She climbed inside and closed the passenger door. "Whatever happened to that oven? Addy would probably get a kick out of making tiny cookies and cakes for us tomorrow. Is it in your parents' attic?"

"No." I started the vehicle, using the wipers to clear the almost half-inch of snow built up off the windshield. "Susan played with it when I was spending the night with you a few weeks later and Dad had to trash it afterward." That oven had gone the way of many of my toys thanks to Susan.

"Why? Did she break it like everything else of yours?"

"She baked a dead mouse in it that she found flattened under a board in the garage." The little shit had sworn she didn't realize that baking the mummified critter would ruin my oven, but the smirk on her face when the garbage truck came the next day proved otherwise in my nine-year-old opinion.

"Eww! What's wrong with that girl?"

That was the question Natalie and I had both asked too many times to count over the years about the Bitch from Hell when it came to her crimes against nature and me. Especially me.

I held my hands over the vents in the dash, warming my fingers. "Well, Dr. Freud, I'd sum it up as Susan is bad to the bone."

Natalie grunted. "She's so mean she'd steal the nickels off a dead man's eyes."

I chuckled and threw out one of Harvey's lines. "Sure as a bear has hair."

My cell phone rang from inside my purse, making me cringe. *What now, Mother?* I fished it out, breathing a sigh of relief at the sight of Doc's name.

I answered with, "If you're calling to spur me along, cowboy, I'm about five minutes away from swinging by your spread and making room for you next to me in my wagon."

"I'm glad to hear it, but you need to stop at work first."

"Why?" I frowned out the window. The snow was coming down so hard now that it was covering the windshield within seconds. The urge to hit the road had my chest growing tight.

"Cornelius just called me."

Cornelius Curion was a paranormal investigator who currently lived above Calamity Jane Realty's office. While he called himself a ghost whisperer, he was really more of an ectoplasmic magnet, drawing wispy followers out of the woodwork. Doc and I shared custody of the eccentric Pied Piper of ghosts, meaning that while Cornelius slept in my building, many of his expensive paranormal gadgets and monitors were set up next door in Doc's office for reasons

I didn't want to think about at the moment.

"Why did he call?" I asked. "Does he need your help with something down in Nevada?"

Cornelius had gone to Las Vegas where his super-duper rich family lived. He'd mentioned something about driving out to the desert to visit an old friend in a ghost town called Gold-something. Goldtown? No, Goldwash, that was it. Maybe he had a ghost question for Doc, whose first-hand expertise on the spectral world far overshadowed anyone else I knew.

"He's not in Nevada," Doc answered.

"He's not?"

"No. He's currently one floor above your office."

What? "I thought he went home for the holidays."

"He mentioned a problem with his flight."

"Is that why he called you?"

"No. The spare key I gave him for my office has disappeared. Can you swing by his place on your way here and give him your key for now?"

"Sure. Add another few minutes to our ETA."

" 'Our'? Did you pick up a hitchhiker?"

"Worse. Natalie is coming with us."

"Good. It didn't feel right without her. See you soon, Killer."

I hung up and shifted into gear. "We need to swing by my office and give Cornelius a key. He somehow lost his."

"A Christmas Eve mystery, how intriguing." Natalie buckled her seatbelt. "What's Corny still doing in town?"

"Doc said he had a problem with his flight."

I rolled slowly through the thick slush, taking it easy on the narrow street. There was no rushing in Deadwood when it snowed. The neighborhoods had been built back during the horse and wagon days, so many of the streets were barely wide enough in spots to fit a single modern-day vehicle thanks to the line of parked cars hugging foundation walls and built-in garages along one side. The sheer, stomach-clenching drop to the buildings below on the other side didn't allow much room for error.

If Cornelius was in town, I could kill two birds with one stone and give him the gift I'd picked up for him.

"Do me a favor," I said to Natalie. "Reach in that bag in the back seat and grab the present with silver and white stripes."

She did as requested and pulled out the box. "What's this?"

"A present for Cornelius."

"Ah. I gave him mine the other day because I thought he was leaving."

"What did you give him?" I eased down the hill toward Main Street. The snow was over an inch deep on the sidewalks by now. I grimaced as I hit the brakes to stop for the light. Thankfully, my tires didn't lose traction.

Interstate 90 should be relatively clear still, especially with the plows and salt trucks. However, making it down twisty US Highway 14A to the entrance ramp could prove to be a slight challenge now. At this rate, we might need to chain up before heading out of town.

"I found a travel toiletry kit with a Bigfoot Spotting Crew emblem on the sides that reminded me of him."

I grinned. "I think Bigfoot might be his second cousin."

A couple of minutes later, I pulled into the parking lot behind Calamity Jane Realty. There were no tire tracks in the snow back here, with the lot empty of any signs of life. The slush felt thicker, more slippery, too.

"I dare you to do a doughnut," Natalie said.

As tempting as it was, I resisted. "I'll spin a doughnut if you promise to bribe Detective Cooper with sex when he catches me mid-spin and threatens to lock me away in the hoosegow until next year."

"No way. I'm on sabbatical, especially from the likes of

Coop and his ripped chest and bullet-scarred bod …" She trailed off for a moment, then took a sudden breath, shaking her head quickly. "Besides, that man needs to chill. He's so tense these days. I swear if he sneezes, he'll probably shatter into tiny, razor-sharp pieces."

I glanced her way, noticing that the sad lines around her mouth and eyes were back. Cooper wasn't the only one with his nerves poking through his skin as of late.

"He's tired," I reminded her, defending the prickly detective. In spite of Cooper's tendency to bite me on the ass, I felt sorry for the overstressed law dog. He'd been putting in a lot of extra hours at work so that others on the force could enjoy holiday time with their families. "All of those long shifts he's been pulling have him stuck in Mr. Hyde mode."

"That's 'Detective' Hyde to you, Parker," Natalie said in a low voice, imitating the crotchety detective.

I chuckled. "Have you been practicing his lines in the mirror?"

A shadow passed over her face as she stared out the windshield toward the back of Calamity Jane's building. "I've been thinking about Coop way too much. I should probably take a break."

Natalie and Cooper had almost played hide the lollipop years back. What had started out as a flirty game of pool at the Purple Door Saloon in downtown Deadwood had turned into a heavy-duty makeout session behind the bar. But somewhere between getting acquainted with each other's red zones and actual penetration, Cooper received a call from work that acted as a bucket of ice water on their whole steamy scene. He made the mistake that night of choosing work over Natalie. To make an even bigger mess of their brief affair, the bonehead later popped any feelings Natalie had bubbling to the surface by telling her that he didn't dally with local girls. Then, the dumbass capped off the whole non-affair with a final "end of story" comment that was branded in Natalie's brain.

Now Cooper had gone and changed his mind. He wanted Natalie in his bed and not just for a single romp. He was thinking about breakfast the next morning, too—as in a repeat performance indefinitely. When I'd pressed him on how long he thought this Natalie-urge of his might last, he didn't have an answer. Unfortunately for Cooper, Natalie was standing tall behind her sabbatical-from-men decision, kicking and karate-chopping any feelings that were trying to sway her toward embracing the hard-headed detective again.

"What kind of a break are we talking here?" I prodded her. Being nosy was one of my duties as her best friend. "Like joining a convent and disappearing for a year?"

She smirked. "Do I look like convent material to you?"

I took in her worn overalls, Rudolph the Reindeer scarf, and red stocking cap with a green poof ball on the top. "No. More like a hillbilly variety show guest star."

She made a face at me.

I grinned back. "Even more so now. All you're missing is a piece of straw sticking out of your mouth."

"I'm going to stick a piece of straw somewhere south of your bellybutton if you keep making fun of my Christmas outfit." While I giggled, she sobered. "Actually, I was thinking more along the lines of taking a break from Deadwood and heading down to Jackrabbit Junction for a week or two with my cousins."

Natalie's cousins were the rabble-rousing Morgan sisters whom I'd lived next to in Rapid City while growing up. Even when they were young, the three fireballs had a knack for hunting trouble with a big gun, and when they found it, kicking ass until someone's teeth fell out.

"Knowing the shenanigans Claire, Kate, and Ronnie tend to get mixed up in," I said, "I'm sure some time with them would get your mind off men."

"And probably land me in the pokey down there while I'm at it."

"That, too." I squeezed her hand. "Come on, let's go give Cornelius my present and Doc's key so we can hit the road before it takes stealing a snowplow to escape the hills."

Natalie and I trekked through the snow to the back door leading to the second floor of Calamity Jane Realty's office building. We kicked the slush off our boots on the downstairs mat and then tromped up the stairs with plenty of commotion so Cornelius would hear us coming.

At the top of the stairs, I could hear polka music throbbing through the door.

I knocked hard, trying to make myself heard over the trumpets and accordions.

He didn't answer.

"Now what?" I asked the slab of wood. Maybe I could just slip the key under the door.

Natalie reached around me and turned the knob. The door swung open. "How about that, brainiac?"

"Showoff." I hesitated on the threshold. "Knowing Cornelius, he might be running around naked." Seeing the Abe Lincoln doppelganger's nether regions would probably melt my eyeballs.

"Please," Natalie said. "If you've seen one penis, you've seen them all."

I gawked at her. "Not true. I've seen my fair share of jangly bits both up close and in movies, and so far each one has been like a snowflake."

Her lips twitched. "You mean cold and wet?"

I wrinkled my nose. "I mean unique, smartass. Maybe we need to look into getting you some glasses. This sabbatical from sex may be affecting your vision." I held my hand up in front of her face. "How many fingers am I holding up?"

She knocked my hand away. "My vision is fine. But if

we don't stop that damned polka music, my ears are going to bleed." Natalie led the way inside.

I followed, wincing at the music blaring throughout the large, open studio apartment.

"Cornelius!" I yelled above the yodeling.

Natalie rushed to the stereo and turned it off. "Try again."

I moved to the closed bathroom door, hearing the sound of the shower running on the other side. "Cornelius?" I called.

The water turned off. Shower curtain rings rattled.

"Brace yourself," I warned Natalie and pounded on the bathroom door. I squinted as I waited, hoping to avoid the sight of his bare twig and berries. "Cornelius, it's Violet. I brought you Doc's other spare key."

"Violet who?" he called through the door.

I rolled my eyes. He and I had played this knock-knock game before, usually at the butt crack of dawn at an ear-ringing decibel level through my cell phone. He knew damned well who I was. "I also brought you a present."

The door opened so fast that I yipped and jumped back.

"A present, you say?"

I winced in anticipation of an eyeful of Cornelius in his birthday suit, but he walked out fully dressed in black jeans and a bright orange sweater, smelling minty fresh. His goatee appeared less pointy than usual, but his bright cornflower blue eyes were as sharp as ever.

I scratched my head. "How'd you do that?"

"Do what?"

"Get dressed so fast."

"What makes you think I'm dressed?"

"But … I …" Shaking off my stupor, I gave up. "You know what, never mind."

"I heard there was a problem with your flight to Vegas," Natalie said, setting his present that she'd carried for me on the café-style table in his kitchen alcove.

"Not the flight."

"What then?" I asked.

"The numbers."

I followed him to the kitchen. "You mean the flight times?"

"No, the flight numbers. They were unlucky."

I crossed my arms. "You mean you cancelled your trip home because you didn't like the flight's numbers?"

"Of course," he said it as if that were a common happenstance with airline travelers.

"Why did you book it in the first place if you didn't like the numbers?" I had a feeling I was tumbling down a rabbit hole here, but I couldn't seem to stop myself.

"My original flight was changed. The new numbers were unacceptable, so I opted out of flying to my death and decided to hole up here among Deadwood's ghosts for the time being."

In other words, he was going to stay in this apartment for Christmas. Alone. Well, alone if you didn't count any spirits that might be swirling about.

My heart smarted at the forlorn image of Cornelius sitting in front of his bank of monitors for the next couple of days while the snow piled up outside. Who would go get him his favorite protein drinks if he ran out?

He pointed at the box Natalie had set on the table. "What's that?"

I picked it up and held it out to him. "Your present. Open it."

His brow wrinkled. "What's the occasion?"

"I was aiming for Christmas."

"That's the one with the flying reindeer, right?"

"And the big guy in the red suit. Do you not celebrate Christmas?" Hadn't he been planning to fly home for the holidays? Maybe he celebrated Hanukkah or Kwanza or something else related to the Voodoo religion since his grandmother had been a renowned seer from Louisiana. Or maybe, based on his Halloween-like outfit, he didn't partake in any of the holidays this time of year.

"In the past, yes." He took the present from me.

"Why don't you celebrate it anymore?" Natalie asked.

"The dead don't like to be reminded of this particular holiday." He tore off a strip of the wrapping paper.

I glanced around, wondering if we had any ghostly visitors watching us at this moment. While I had my moments in the paranormal sun here and there, most days I was in the dark when it came to actually being able to spot a ghost.

My focus returned to him. "What about the living?"

He shrugged and tore off more of the paper. "I imagine some of them don't like to be reminded of the horrors that come with Christmas either."

Horrors? I snorted. He must have spent a holiday with my sister at some point.

"When I say 'the living,' I mean you." I tapped his chest. "You're still alive, aren't you?"

"That depends."

Natalie shot me a grin. "On what, Cornelius? The time of day?"

"To which part of my body you are referring in this case. For example, my hair shafts are dead cells."

"Isn't the top layer of your skin dead, too?" she asked.

"If you're referring to the thicker, horny layer, that's a common misperception. It's still alive and quite useful."

Natalie guffawed. "My horny layer is way too much alive these days. It doesn't seem to understand that the rest of us are on sabbatical."

"I know someone who would be happy to fix that problem for you," I reminded her.

Her gaze narrowed. "That would turn my little problem

into a calamity of epic proportions, and you know it."

I did. Unfortunately for Natalie, her heart usually led the way into relationships and ended up battered, bruised, and curled up in a gutter.

Turning back to Cornelius, I tapped on the unwrapped box he held in his hands. "Open it."

He lifted the lid. "What is this?" He extracted the maroon material.

"A new robe," I said, taking the empty box from him so he could hold up the thick, soft robe. "Your yellow one has seen better days." Not to mention it was too short for my viewing comfort. This new one would cover his hairy knees. I had Doc try it on to double-check its length.

Cornelius lowered the robe. "Does this mean I can walk around without trousers in your presence now?"

"No. I still require pants at all times in your case."

"That's unfortunate." He set the robe on the table next to the empty box. "Thank you for the gift, Violet. I will think of you every time I wear it."

I grimaced. That wasn't quite what I'd been going for.

"I have something for you as well," he said, walking over to a narrow door next to the bathroom. "Or rather, for your son."

He did? "You do?"

"This arrived yesterday." He pulled out a trident that was almost as tall as me. "I believe you'll want it for tomorrow's festivities, although it might be a tight fit under the tree."

"Is that real?" Natalie asked, joining him. She ran her finger down the steel shaft.

"As real as you're going to find in this century. It was made by a weaponsmith who specializes in medieval bronze and steel weaponry."

I stepped closer, admiring the swirling designs etched into the forked head. Layne was going to flip his lid over this. His list for Santa had been a mishmash of weapons, helmets, and books about both, but ... "Cornelius, I don't know if I can afford this."

"I thought money was no object for you," he said.

A shout of laughter escaped my lips before I could corral it. "What makes you think that?"

"You rarely carry cash and wear expensive shoes."

Natalie smiled. "He's got you nailed, babe."

"Not quite. I don't carry cash most days because supporting two children on my own sucks the lifeblood out of my wallet." I ran my fingertips over the tallest of the three metal points on the head. "As for my shoes, my mother supports my addiction to pricey footwear." Her generosity to my feet was part of why I had put up with Susan's shit for as long as I had. As much as I would like to shove a mummified mouse down her gullet and set her out for the garbage truck to take, I didn't want to piss off my shoe supplier.

Okay, truth be told, it went way deeper than that with

my mom, including a smidgeon of parental-induced guilt and a dollop of unconditional love, but the expensive shoes Mom routinely gave me went a long way toward healing Susan's claw scratches.

Cornelius held out the trident for me to take. "Don't worry about the cost. I'll make a trade with you."

"I'm not sure I have anything you want."

"Not want, but need."

I took the trident, my eyes narrowing. "What's that?"

"A strong connection with a certain changeling ghost."

Not that again. I sighed. "So, you'll give me this undoubtedly very expensive trident in exchange for channeling an evil child ghost that could make my life hell if I screw up during the process and allow it to latch onto me like a ghoulish tick?"

"When you put it that way, yes."

I looked to Natalie for guidance, being that she had several extra months of experience over me in age. "What do you think I should do, oh wise one?"

She shrugged.

That was it. Nothing else.

"Golly gee, Nat. Your brilliance is blinding me."

She flipped me off. "Can you see that through my brilliance?"

"That's it. I'm telling Santa on you."

To Cornelius, I said, "Fine. It's a deal." I would've probably been roped into channeling the ghost brat one way or another, since Doc was on Cornelius's side when it came to ensnaring the wily changeling. Before Cornelius could say anything, I blurted, "On one condition."

"What's the condition?" Natalie asked, sounding like his attorney.

"Are you working for him or me?"

"Him," she said, her eyes alight, teasing. "He's agreed to teach me how to get guys to treat me better."

He did? Was that why she'd given him the shaving kit? Had it been another trade deal? Was this guidance supposed to help her fight off her feelings for Cooper, or was it intended for men in general?

I pushed aside my questions for later when she and I were alone. "My condition is that Cornelius comes to my parents' place with us for the holiday."

I had an idea that would keep Cornelius from staying home alone in this apartment over Christmas while at the same time giving him a purpose so he didn't feel like a third wheel.

Cornelius cocked his head to the side. "This seems like a courtship ritual of some sort. I don't believe your Tall Medium would approve of me posing as your love companion again in front of your parents."

"It's not a courtship ritual, so don't worry about my Tall Medium. Doc will be there with us. This is more of a defensive move since my sister will also be there and she has a history of pawing you all over."

"But wasn't that when Susan had Cornelius confused for Doc and was trying to make you jealous?"

"Yes," I told Natalie. "But Cornelius has a way of throwing Susan off her game. He might be able to run interference for me."

"So, in addition to giving you the trident," Natalie clarified, "Cornelius has to try to distract the man-stealing tramp for a couple of days?"

"Bingo. Between his efforts and yours, I'm hoping Susan won't be able to connive my demise as easily."

Natalie frowned. "Sheesh, you're not taking any chances this time, are you?"

"Never underestimate the power of the Bitch from Hell. Mark my words, her forked tongue has wreaked havoc for the last time on my love life."

"Your littermate has a forked tongue?" Cornelius asked.

"Metaphorically speaking."

He stroked his beard. "I've often wondered what it would be like to exchange saliva in a French fashion with someone whose tongue is split in two."

Natalie and I both blinked at him, no words coming forth from either of us for several beats.

"What do you think?" he asked Natalie.

"Well, based on decades of dealing with Violet's sister, you're getting the shaft in this deal."

I poked her in the shoulder. "Remind me to ask Santa for a new best friend for Christmas next year."

She poked me back. "You'll be lucky to get a tiny lump of coal with the way you're going, Executioner."

She had a point. While selling real estate was harmless enough most days, my part-time job of killing otherworldly assholes was sure to put me at the top of the Naughty list along with Susan … if I lived that long. Executing deadly troublemakers was a hazardous business.

"How many nights?" Cornelius asked me.

"Only two." I hoped.

"You'd better pack for three," Natalie chimed in like a death knoll.

I squinted at her for *not* helping. She wrinkled her nose back at me.

"What's your parents' house number?" Cornelius asked.

"3731. Why?"

"Prime numbers. Most excellent." Handing me the trident, he said, "Since I'm already prepared for an extended stay away, I agree to the terms of your deal, Violet."

He picked up his bag that sat next to the Murphy bed in the living room and then detoured to the bathroom, returning with a shaving kit that had a Bigfoot emblem on the side. He stuffed the kit and his new robe in his bag. "What is the destination location for this holiday event?"

"Rapid City." I held up the key that had instigated our

visit with Cornelius. "I guess you won't be needing Doc's key now."

He took it and pocketed it. "Not until I return from completing my diversion duties with your littermate." He shut off the lights and indicated for us to lead the way out of the apartment.

Natalie opened the door. "What happened to your key, Cornelius?"

I followed her down the stairs, trident in hand. "Did you lose it?"

"Violet's dead boss hid it from me."

I did an about-face, frowning up at him as he closed the door.

Natalie waited for us at the base of the stairs. "How could Jane's ghost hide your key to Doc's office?"

Actually, the "how" of it wasn't so much of a question, since Jane had been growing more active over the last month or two. My dead boss was the reason Cornelius had been asked to move into the apartment above our office in the first place. However, ever since Cornelius had started sharing space with Jane's ghost, her abilities had strengthened to worrisome levels.

"The better question in this case," I said, "is *why* would Jane hide the key from you?"

He hitched his bag over his shoulder. "She's averse to me watching her through my video cameras."

"Did she whisper that in your ear or something?" Natalie pressed.

"She made her feelings clear via the whiteboard in Violet's office this morning." Cornelius started down the stairs toward me.

That was fitting. Jane always had a penchant for filling the office whiteboards with to-do lists.

"What did she write?" I asked.

"Stop watching me!"

Chapter Five

Maybe I was overreacting about Susan having diabolical plans to steal my boyfriend, but she was slippery as a pocket full of pudding. If I could stack the deck in my favor with the aid of Natalie and Cornelius, I might not find myself squirming like a worm in hot ashes throughout the next couple of days of holiday merriments.

My phone rang as soon as I crawled behind the steering wheel in my SUV. I pulled it out as Natalie piled in next to me, her stocking cap and coat heavily sprinkled with snow from the short rush across the parking lot. Cornelius took the back seat.

A glance at the phone's screen confirmed my fears—my mother was calling yet again, undoubtedly to remind me that the sky was still falling in frozen wet pieces.

I handed Natalie my phone as I started the engine. "Answer that for me, would you?"

"Sure thing." She held the phone to her ear. "Santa's workshop, Natalie the drunken elf speaking."

I heard my mom's laughter coming through the line, followed by a flurry of words. Shifting into drive, I headed out of the lot. According to the Honda's external thermometer, the temperature had dropped noticeably outside over the last half hour. The parking lot had a slight crunch underneath the snow where there used to be slush.

Natalie smiled as she listened. My parents had unofficially adopted my best friend as one of their own long ago, including Natalie in our family holiday plans since we were kids. Not having her with us at all this year would have been odd.

"Yeah, she's right here next to me trying to drive through this mess," she told my mom.

My tires lost traction for a second or two when I pulled out onto Sherman Street. The snowplow had recently been through on the main drag, but Old Man Winter was making quick work of whiting out the plow's hard work.

"I know, it's crazy," Natalie continued. "We'll be on our way as soon as we pick up Doc." She paused, listening. "*We* as in Vi, Doc, Cornelius, and me." Another pause. Natalie grinned at me. "Yes, Cornelius is the one who talked about his dead grandfather's fondness for coffin flies at the family dinner a few weeks ago." She listened again and laughed, glancing back at Cornelius. "No, I don't believe he's ever been employed by a traveling circus. However, I have been recently informed that one of his female ancestors was revered as some sort of voodoo queen down in the Louisiana swampland."

A cacophony of squawks and high-pitched utterances came through the line.

Natalie held the phone away, snorting and giggling. Her lips were still twitching at the corners when she returned to the call. "Is Cornelius coming as my date? No. He's a good friend. Your daughter insisted he come along with us because he couldn't make it home to his family for the holidays due to a flight issue."

I heard my mom's compassionate "ohhh" through the line. Damn, Natalie was good. She knew all about my mom's soft spot for orphaned souls.

I passed a few other four-wheel drive vehicles as well as a pair of snowmobiles as I steered through the mess to Doc's house, a few blocks away from the office. If it weren't for Doc, a new set of chains, and four-wheel drive, I would have been doing more knuckle chewing about making the snowy drive to my parents.

As we neared Doc's, I whispered to Natalie, "Wrap it

up."

Natalie nodded at me. "Was there something you needed from Violet?" she asked my mom in a much nicer way than I would have at this point. Her forehead furrowed, her smile flipping into a troubled frown. "Sure thing, Hope-ster. I'll let her know. Don't worry, we'll be there raiding your fridge before long. Give Susan my love and tell her I'll see her soon."

I giggled. That should get Susan good and spooked. Natalie's historic feats of retaliation against her on my account were almost as legendary as Susan's evil deeds.

Natalie hung up after saying good-bye. She tucked the phone back in my purse. "Your mom needs a bottle of tequila."

I guffawed, pulling in behind the Picklemobile, an old green truck Doc was borrowing from Harvey while he stored his souped-up 1969 Camaro SS in his garage. "That's why she called? She's low on liquor?" Hell, I wasn't even there yet to get the mayhem rolling. I shut off the engine.

"No. She called because she just heard on the news that they closed Interstate 90 from the Wyoming border to Rapid City."

"Fudgesicles!" I groaned, leaning my head on the steering wheel. Now what?

Cornelius spoke up from the back seat. "Truth be told, I actually spent a summer working for a circus troupe during college."

"Really?" Natalie turned to look at him. "Doing what?"

"Training the monkeys to ride unicycles."

A bubble of laughter rose up my throat, hilarity and hysteria mixing in my chest.

Damned the meteorologists for being right this time.

How in the hell was I going to get to my kids?

Natalie patted my back. "We'll figure out a way to Rapid," she said, reading my mind. "Let's go talk to Doc.

He and his big brain will have a solution."

The three of us scurried around Harvey's Ford pickup that sat next to the Picklemobile and climbed the steps onto Doc's front porch.

The door opened before I could knock. Harvey ushered us inside, shutting out the wind that was trying to beat down the door. Green and white striped suspenders were hooked to his jeans, looking festive with his red flannel shirt.

"You're cuttin' it close, Sparky," he said, frowning at me through his salt-and-pepper beard. His matching eyebrows were wrinkled into one long bushy caterpillar. "A blizzard is a bad time to be drivin' through the backside of nowhere."

"What do you mean, the backside of nowhere?" I unbuttoned my coat and then took off my cable knit beanie, shaking out my damp blond curls.

"They shut down Interstate 90 clear to Rapid."

"We heard," Natalie said, tugging off her stocking hat.

"The only way yer gonna git home now is up Strawberry Hill on Highway 385 and out past my ranch."

Natalie sucked air through her teeth. "That's a lot of twists and turns and hills to slip and slide through. We could try Nemo Road, but it might be even worse and your parents live closer to where Rimrock Highway dumps us into Rapid."

"Those flying reindeer would come in handy right about now," Cornelius said, stuffing his gloves in his coat pockets. He sniffed. "What's that divine aroma?"

"Chocolate peanut butter surprise cookies," Harvey answered. "Feel free to help yerself to some. They're on the counter."

Cornelius didn't hesitate, his long legs speeding toward Doc's kitchen.

"US 385 is tricky in the snow," I said, returning to the problem at hand. "But it's still doable."

I spoke from experience. My dad had driven us home from Aunt Zoe's place through the snow many times in the past.

"Sure," Natalie said, rubbing her hands together. "If the plows are still running up there."

"Are they?" I asked Harvey.

Harvey scratched at his beard. "Let me call Coop and double-check."

"Where is Coop?" Natalie asked, earning a pair of raised brows from me. She ignored me, focusing extra hard on Harvey. "I thought he was going to his mom's place for the holiday."

"He's still at work."

"Of course Detective Scrooge is still hunched over his desk," Natalie grumbled. "He'll probably work straight through Christmas and not even realize it."

Natalie suffered from a twisted sort of professional jealousy when it came to Cooper's job, stemming from his choosing to run away to his work rather than finishing what he started with her that night behind the Purple Door Saloon.

"Knock it off, Grinch," I told her. "You're raining bitterness all over my Merry freakin' Christmas."

While I understood the pain of rejection, Natalie needed to move on with her life and focus on the here and now—such as how in the hell we were going to make it to my kids down in Rapid City.

She harrumphed. "Fine. If you need me, my sour puss will be in the kitchen scarfing down a plateful of cookies."

As she followed in Cornelius's wake, I looked around. "Where's Doc?"

Harvey thumbed toward the stairs. "He told me to send ya up when ya got here."

I checked to make sure my boots were clear of snow and started up the stairs.

"Hold up, Sparky. Coop wanted me to give you something."

"Coop?" I hesitated. "Is it an orange jumpsuit and a set of chained ankle cuffs?"

Harvey rooted around in the closet beneath the stairs. He came out with a Christmas present the size of a large clothing box and handed it to me.

"What's this?"

"Coop said ya wanted it fer yer stallion."

"Ohhhh." I smiled, knowing what was in the box now. Cooper had come through on one of my gifts for Doc. "Did your nephew actually wrap this?" The box even had a pretty bow and ribbon curls.

" 'Course not. I did."

I kissed Harvey's cheek. "You're the best bodyguard around. Save me some cookies before Natalie and Cornelius hog them all."

I hurried up the stairs, knocking lightly on the bedroom door before opening it. "Doc?"

He stood on the other side of his bed at his desk, wearing black jeans and the brown sweater that turned his eyes into dark chocolate bliss. One smolder from him while wearing that sweater would rocket my head to the North Pole, no reindeer needed.

Doc's focus remained on his laptop screen as I shut the door. "Come take a look at this, Killer."

I crossed to his desk, setting the present down on his bed before joining him. I touched his back as I leaned down to look at the screen. The urge to slide my cold fingers under his soft sweater and let him warm me up in more ways than one made me lean toward him and breathe him in. He smelled tempting, a mixture of Harvey's cookies and spicy cologne. The combination had part of me wanting to nibble on his neck and the other wanting to jump his bones.

I settled for a kiss on his beard-stubbled jaw before

zeroing in on the weather radar map displayed on his laptop. As I watched, the image on the screen shifted through the past twenty minutes, showing the storm move in five-minute intervals over the northern Black Hills.

"I take it you heard about Interstate 90," I said, scowling at all of the snow-inspired blues and purples on the screen.

"Yep." Doc pointed at US Highway 385 on the screen. "The thick of the storm hasn't shifted too far south yet, but it's heading in that direction. We need to leave soon. According to the latest weather report, it will engulf all of the northern hills in the next few hours."

"Crud." I blew out a breath. "We should probably grab a shovel and pack some food along to be safe."

He took a step back from his desk. "You still have that box of litter in the back of your Honda? We might need it to help with traction."

I nodded, pulling my gaze away from the screen to find him down staring at me with an expression I couldn't quite read. I stood upright. "What? Do I have something on my face?"

He tugged on one of my curls. "You look cute with your pink nose and matching cheeks." His gaze drifted south. "I really like those purple snow boots."

So he'd mentioned several times since I bought them a few days ago. "You have purple boots on the brain."

The corners of his eyes crinkled. "Always."

"It's freezing out there."

"I know how to heat you up, *cara mia*." He slid his hand around to the back of my neck and bent down, warming my lips for starters.

"There's no time," I whispered and went up on my toes, wrapping my arms around his neck. I kissed a path along his stubble-covered jaw to his earlobe. "I have a present for you, *mon cher*."

"Ah, Tish." He gripped my hips, pulling me closer. "If it's you naked in my bed with another red ribbon and more sweet torture in your plans, then I must be on Santa's Nice list this year."

"Oh, you've been nice." I tugged playfully on his earlobe with my teeth. "Really nice, and extra good, too. But that present comes later, after we make it through the storm and are under the covers in my old bedroom."

"Your parents are going to let me sleep in the same bed with you?"

I laughed, pulling back to look up at him. "Are you serious?"

"Sure." His gaze dipped to my lips. "They might worry that I'll ravish their daughter in her childhood boudoir."

"Ravish? That's all you're planning to do? And here I was hoping to be scandalously seduced and led sinfully astray, my innocence plucked and plundered."

"Really?" He kissed me again. I swayed toward him, taking the reins, my tongue teasing his. After several pulse-pounding seconds, he pulled back, a smirk on his mouth. "*Innocence*, you say? You don't kiss like a maiden, milady."

"A maiden?" I gave a bawdy tavern-wench laugh while picking up the present I'd brought upstairs with me. "Mister, I'd take up with a snake if it promised me a good time." I held out the gift.

He chuckled. "You've been hanging around Harvey too much, saucy wench." He took the present. "What's this?"

"Open it and see."

"It's not Christmas yet."

"This is a private gift for our eyes only."

One dark eyebrow cocked. "If it's a skin-tight leather getup with a ball gag, I'm not wearing it unless you have a matching one."

I grinned. "Just open it."

He peeled off the ribbon and paper. When he lifted the

lid, his eyes widened. "Where did you get this?"

"I had a little help with my shopping from a certain law dog. He guarantees it'll do the job."

Doc pulled the Kevlar vest from the box, holding it up to admire it. "It's lighter than it looks."

"Made with some of the newest technology, or so I'm told." Cooper had assured me it would do the job of keeping Doc safer during our hunts—or rather haunts.

He slid it on, fastening it over his chest. Cooper had been spot on with the size for Doc. I stood and knocked on the material over his heart. "Rock solid, just like the sexy stud underneath it."

Doc caught my wrist. "I'm not sure if I should be flattered or scared by this gift. What do you have planned for me, Killer?"

I winked. "What can I say? I like really rough foreplay. I'd hate for you to get hurt before you finish the job."

"You and me both." He lifted my hand, his lips brushing my knuckles. "Thank you. I'll wear it on our next date."

I sat down on the bed as he unfastened the vest and slid it off, placing it next to me on the comforter. I scratched my fingernails down the front. "Cooper says he wears his over a white T-shirt most days, especially when he knows he'll be hanging around me."

"Yet you still find ways to bruise the poor guy." Doc walked over to his closet. "At least you won't be able to pinch me in as many places when I'm wearing it." He opened one of the closet doors. "I have a little something for you, too. Close your eyes."

I did as told, resisting the urge to peek. My heart pounded. If he was holding an engagement ring when I opened my eyes, I was going to keel over. Marriage was a subject I avoided like the plague with Doc, even though he'd recently informed me that he was not allergic to wearing matching gold bands. A bachelor of thirty-nine years may claim that talk of getting hitched doesn't give him the hives, but I wasn't merely a single woman looking for a partner to go to dinner and the movies with once a week during date night. I had two kids who needed a dad. My overloaded Conestoga wagon might be more trouble than he bargained for once we settled into riding the trail together for the long term.

"Okay, open them," Doc said.

I did and gasped.

It was not a little square box with a sparkly ring.

Not even close.

"What's that?" I stared at what looked like a bat with an array of four-inch-long metal spikes poking out of one end. The handle had a leather grip with steel flanges above and below it to keep it from slipping free in the thick of battle—a detail Cooper would appreciate the next time we took turns swinging and shooting at sharp-toothed troublemakers.

"It's a mace," Doc answered. "I found a blacksmith south of Hill City who makes custom weapons."

Was this the same guy who'd made the trident?

"I told him my idea and he brought it to life." Doc held it out for me to take. "Try out your new weapon, Killer."

I gripped the mace. The leather-wrapped neck was soft to the touch, like it had been worked and worn for comfort. I smiled up at him, my heart swelling. "You got me a custom-made spiky bat," I said huskily, my throat tight with emotion. It was the perfect weapon to make me feel better after I lost my war hammer. "That's so romantic!"

His cheeks darkened a smidgeon, his gaze lowering to the bat. "I've watched you work a war hammer and a crowbar. While you were good with both, I thought you might be even better with something more like a softball bat, being that you were an all-star player in high school."

I choked up with the mace, like I was standing at home plate facing off with an invisible pitcher, and swung. The weapon felt solid in my hands, the heft of it weighted perfectly for me. I took another swing, forward and back.

"Damn, this is sweet." I glanced down at the Kevlar vest then at Doc, who was leaning against his desk watching me with one hell of a smolder in his eyes. "Why don't you suit up, Candy Cane, and let me take a swing or two at you."

He laughed. "Nice try, Killer, but my ribs are still healing from our rendezvous in Slagton."

I lowered the mace, my smile slipping at the reminder of his sore ribs. "You sure you want to go down the mountain today? Maybe you need to stay home and rest."

His brow lowered. "Are you looking for an excuse to go to your family's Christmas without me?"

"No. Of course not." I thought about it for another second and answered more honestly. "Okay, maybe. The idea of spending several days with my sister sniffing around you has me sweating. I'm antsy about ending up with a serious case of heartburn for the holidays."

"Heartburn, nice." He got my play on words. "I told you not to worry about Susan. I have eyes for only you."

"But I'm not tall, thin, and gorgeous. She's like kinky sex on a popsicle stick."

"Violet, I am so nuts about you that I gave you a lethal weapon for Christmas. A custom mace is not the sort of gift a guy buys for just any girl, you know."

I dropped the mace on the bed next to his Kevlar vest and crossed to him, settling between his legs. I slid my hands around his waist, hugging him while I stared up at him with my heart in my eyes. "Thank you, Doc."

"Trust me, Boots," he said, using the nickname reserved for the stolen moments when we were usually alone and naked—well, naked except for my purple cowboy boots.

"From the tips of your wild curls to the ends of your adorable toes, you are sexy as hell. I'm a man who appreciates curves, and you, fair maiden, make my knees go weak whenever I see you. You were made for me." He ran the back of his fingers down my cheek and then followed with his lips. "And my mouth."

"And your hands." I nuzzled his neck, his beard stubble tickling my nose as his hands cupped and squeezed my backside. "Do we have to stay in Rapid for more than one night?"

"I don't think this storm is giving us any choice."

I kissed his Adam's apple and stepped back. "Okay. I'm bringing reinforcements just in case, though."

"You mean Natalie?"

"And Cornelius."

"Cornelius agreed to come along?"

I winced. "I kind of shanghaied him into coming, too. He was going to stay alone in that apartment for Christmas." At the twitch of Doc's lips, I added, "And Jane's being mean to him. She hid your key."

"Did she?" He moved to the bed. "Well, I for one am glad he's coming."

"You are?"

"Sure. He'll keep things interesting without even trying." He grabbed the mace and Kevlar vest from the bed. "I'll put these in my closet until we get back to Deadwood."

I went into his bathroom and checked my face in the mirror. There was no hiding my swollen lips or the redness on my cheeks from his beard stubble, but I patted down my curls, anyway, and then followed Doc down the back stairs to the kitchen.

Harvey was pulling a tray of cookies from the oven as we filed out of the narrow stairwell. He looked me over from top to bottom and grinned wide enough for his two gold teeth to show. "Would ya like a cookie after yer

Christmas Eve nookie?"

I pinched his side, making him yip and dance away. I reached for a cookie, risking getting my fingers bit by Cornelius and Natalie, who were guarding a plateful of the chocolate delights like hungry Doberman pinschers.

"What did Cooper say about the roads?" I asked.

"The plows are runnin' up on US 385 as far as he knows." Harvey pulled off his oven mitt. "But he's dead set that you wantin' to drive in this mess confirms his theory that anything north of yer ears is pure snowdrift."

I crossed my arms. "He didn't say that."

"Well, he said somethin' like it." Harvey tossed the mitt on the counter. "Even if the plows are runnin' up Strawberry, there's no guarantee ya won't have to take a detour along the way and end up in the middle of nowhere up to yer hips in snow."

"I know this is a risk, but Santa's presents are in the back of my rig and if I don't make it down there by morning—"

"I know, I know. Yer kids will be eatin' sorrow by the bowlful if you and those presents aren't waitin' fer them when they open their peepers."

"Exactly. So what do I do?"

He untied the "Life's short, moon the cook!" apron that I gave him yesterday for Christmas and draped it over one of the bar stools. "I have just the solution fer ya."

"What's that?"

He hooked his thumbs in his suspenders. "Ya take me along with ya to help play San-ty Claus."

Chapter Six

Today wasn't the first time I'd thought about Susan's demise. Back in eighth grade, I went so far as to plan out her funeral, including the music, flowers, guest list, and type of casket and headstone. I even drew out the layout for the memorial service, seating my parents, brother, and me front and center.

My mistake was writing it all down in my notebook, including the drawing, which my mom found while cleaning out my backpack during Christmas break. I could still picture Mom's pale face and teary eyes when she asked what the memorial layout was. She knew the answer because I'd stupidly written "Susan's Death Celebration" at the top of some of the pages, but she insisted I spell it out for her.

Lesson learned that day: When secretly plotting to eliminate a family member, don't use titles on the funeral schematics.

Those drawings had prompted my mother to contact a counselor for Susan and me. Six months of weekly meetings later, my dad put a stop to it all. A short time after that, I overheard him talking about us to Mom in the garage, eavesdropping through the dog door when they thought they were alone. He could see the writing on the wall. No amount of therapy would ever fix our broken relationship. We might share blood, but we were too different, and both too headstrong. The best they could hope for was a truce until Susan and I were old enough to go our separate ways. The sound of my mother sobbing as he comforted her made my heart hurt, so much so that I vowed that day not to lower myself to Susan's level ever again.

Unfortunately, that vow didn't last.

"You have all of the kids' gifts, right?" Natalie's voice snapped me back to the present.

"Yep. They're tucked away behind the back seat."

I stared at the white world outside Doc's kitchen window. The snow wasn't letting up even a little, and now gusts of wind were adding swirls of icy flurries. Poor Doc and Cornelius were outside putting the chains on my tires, prepping it for the forty-plus mile trip over the river, through the woods, and down the mountain to my parents' place. My fingers were crossed that tire chains would be enough.

Natalie leaned back against the counter next to me. "You killed everything that could spark a fire at your aunt's place, including the Christmas lights, right?"

"Hey, they don't call me an Executioner for nothing," I joked. "I killed everything in Aunt Zoe's fortress but her attraction to Reid Martin," I added, grinning at my own wittiness about my aunt's hot-to-trot old flame, who also happened to be Deadwood's fire captain. "That hunka-hunka burnin' love is hot-wired to spark Aunt Zoe into flames."

Natalie's grin matched mine. "Reid doesn't just ignite sparks in Zoe, he lights her up from head to toe like a five-alarm fire."

A snort of laughter came from the pantry where Harvey was loading crackers and snacks into a tote bag. "Good thing Martin packs his hose wherever he goes so he can put out the fire in yer aunt's pants."

"Oh, sheesh, Harvey," Natalie said. "That was so corny it popped before you finished."

I groaned in agreement.

"What's Reid doing for Christmas, anyway?" she asked me. "Doesn't he have a son somewhere?"

I shrugged. "He's not spending it at my parents' with

Aunt Zoe, that's what." Not after the way my dad bellowed and pawed the ground when Reid showed up at Aunt Zoe's door a few weeks ago, hoping for a spot next to her at the family dinner table. My dad's threat to rearrange Reid's handsome mug for breaking his baby sister's heart wasn't merely a blast of hot air and Aunt Zoe knew it. Dad had been the one she'd leaned on years back when Reid shied away from marrying her. Now the heartbreaker had returned, toting a pack of matches along with a fireman's helmet full of charm, but my dad was ready with his own version of a fire extinguisher—two fists and a hefty rubber boot.

"I thought yer aunt was softenin' up to Cap'n Smokey."

"Oh, she is," I said. "But I think she's got tender spots on the inside that are still frozen solid. Unfortunately, until she tells my dad she's changed her mind about letting Reid light a fire under her heart again, he's going to shoot first when it comes to protecting her."

"Bad luck for Reid," Natalie said. "I've seen your dad work a gun. He's a crack shot. But back to your closing up your aunt's place, what about Duke, Bogart, and Elvis?"

"I made sure they have food and drink to last until …" I frowned in Harvey's direction. "Crud. We have to stop by Aunt Zoe's before we head up Strawberry."

"Why's that?" Harvey asked without looking up.

"I have to get Elvis."

Natalie's eyes narrowed. "What do you mean, 'get' her? Where are you going to take her?"

"With us."

"Horse feathers, Sparky. Cartin' a chicken to Christmas is nuttier than squirrel turds." Harvey stuffed a bag of dried prunes in the tote. "Just fill up the birdy's bowl with plenty of feed and that chicken will be so fat she gets in her own way by the time we get home."

"Sure, Elvis will be fine," I told him. "But Addy will be

a mess once she sees you."

The front door closed, followed by the sound of boots stomping on the doormat. The guys must have the SUV ready to crunch through the snow and ice.

"Vi, you can't be serious about taking that dumb chicken all of the way to your mom's. I know Addy has her leash-trained, but she's not actually a dog."

Cornelius walked into the kitchen, his jacket and black hair glistening with melting snow. "Did you know chickens can produce over thirty different sounds?" he asked Natalie, stealing a cookie from the bag Harvey had filled with the chewy version of chocolate and peanut butter heaven. "They have their own chicken language."

"Thirty, huh?" Natalie guffawed. "That's twenty-nine more sounds than my last boyfriend made during sex."

I laughed. Picturing Natalie's last boyfriend, I didn't doubt her for a second. I turned to Cornelius. "Did you guys get the chains on okay?" I took a cookie from the bag, too, before sealing it and handing it off to Harvey.

Cornelius nodded. "The Tall Medium did most of the work. Southern living hasn't allowed me much experience with snowy weather apparatus."

"Whaddya mean, Addy will be a mess when she sees *me*?" Harvey set the cookies on top of the bag and closed the pantry door. "Makes no sense."

"The only reason we were able to get her down to my parents without that damned chicken was because I told her you would be up here checking on Elvis every day. She trusts you way more than me when it comes to that bird."

Cornelius rubbed his hands together. "Chicken origins have been traced back to theropods."

"What are theropods?" Natalie asked.

"Dinosaurs from the late Triassic period," Doc answered, joining us. Like Cornelius, he was covered with melting snow. "You ready?" he asked me.

"That's over 200 million years ago," Cornelius clarified for Natalie.

"Yeah," I told Doc. To Harvey, I explained, "When you show up with me at my parents' place, Addy will realize that her chicken is on her own for several days and freak out. The whole time we're there, she'll worry incessantly about Elvis being stuck in her cage."

He harrumphed. "So, set Elvis free and let her run around the basement to her heart's content."

"No way! She knows how to open the basement door."

"You're kidding?" Natalie gaped. "Next you'll tell me she learned the dance moves to 'Jail House Rock.' "

"I knew of a chicken named Cluck Berry that could put jigsaw puzzles together," Cornelius told us. "Although the fifty-piece variety was its limit. Anything bigger and it would eat the extra pieces."

I frowned at him for a moment, and then shook my head at Natalie. "I'm not kidding. Given free rein, that damned bird will molt on my comforter and hide eggs all over the house like a feathered Easter bunny."

"What are you suggesting?" Doc asked, his arms crossed as he leaned against the wall. "We take Elvis with us?"

"What if she gets a wild hair and flaps and flutters all over inside your rig?" Natalie threw out. "We don't want her distracting Doc while he's trying to drive through that mess outside."

She had a good point.

"We could stuff 'er in yer tumbleweed wagon," Harvey said.

"My what?"

"Yer puss-n-boots box."

I looked to Doc for help. "Translate, please."

"I think Harvey means Bogart's cat carrier."

Ohhh. "That's actually a good idea."

"I'm full of 'em," the old buzzard said with a shit-eating grin.

"You're full of something, all right," I said, snapping one of his suspenders.

"We need to hit the road," Doc said, grabbing the bag of food at Harvey's feet. "The snow's getting deep fast."

A few minutes later, we filed out the front door. I waited as Doc locked it behind us, leaving his porch light on but the rest of the place dark.

"What about Cooper?" I asked him, feeling bad at the thought of the grumpy detective coming home to a dark house on Christmas Eve.

I really needed to get over this newfound concern for the law dog. More often than not Cooper snapped his teeth at me when I tried to pet him. For some reason, though, I had a feeling that deep inside his barbed wire–wrapped heart hid a lonely flea-sized seed of love waiting to grow.

Then again, I had a history of misjudging men. Case in point, the two shitheads who had easily jumped from my bed into my sister's behind my back.

Doc put his arm around my shoulders as we descended the porch steps. "Last I heard, Coop was staying at his mom's tonight."

"Good." I handed him my keys. "Thanks for driving."

He scowled at the road. "It's going to be ugly going up Strawberry, but the chains should help."

I looked at my SUV. "Is that a trident strapped on my roof?"

"Yep. That was Cornelius's idea."

We all piled into my Honda. Doc and Harvey took the front seats. I scooted into the back seat, playing monkey in the middle between Natalie and Cornelius. Doc backed out of his driveway. We traveled the few blocks to Aunt Zoe's with no problems thanks to a neighbor who had a plow blade on the front of his old Jeep and a love for shoving snow around. In storms like this bugger, the big plows couldn't afford to waste time scraping through the neighborhoods when they had to keep the main roads clear for emergency vehicles.

Natalie ran inside Aunt Zoe's house with me to get Addy's chicken. We returned five minutes later covered with feathers and sporting several peck marks. Elvis squawked from the cat carrier as I stuffed the caged beast in the back and slammed the hatch.

"Damned bird!" I grumbled and raced around to the car door Natalie held open for me.

"Everything go okay in there?" Doc asked, his eyes creased with laughter as he watched me settle in via the rearview mirror.

"Stupid Tyrannosaurus-chicken!" I snarled. "I should have left her there in the dark. That would teach the puny dinosaur a lesson."

"Chickens can actually see better than humans," Cornelius told me as I buckled up. "They have two additional types of cones in their eyes that allow them to distinguish both violet and ultraviolet light."

Harvey snorted. "Doc has a cone that can pick out Violet in the dark, too, don't ya?"

I pinched the old buzzard's arm. "Keep it up and I'll dump you in the snow at the top of Strawberry."

Harvey's snort morphed into a chortle. "I got 'er all hot and bothered fer ya," he told Doc. "Ya owe me one."

I glared at Cornelius. "What's with you and all of this chicken trivia? Did you major in chickens in college or something?"

He plucked a feather from my hair, letting it fall at our feet. "My grandmother had chickens in Louisiana when I was young. *Gallus gallus domesticus* are fascinating to observe during play, particularly when they joust."

Natalie leaned forward to look at him around me.

"Chickens joust?" At his nod, she added, "Like Knights of the Round Table sort of jousting? Or—"

"Stop!" I held up my hands. "There will be no more talk of chickens until we get to Rapid, understand?"

Elvis let out a loud squawk from the back.

I turned in the seat and grabbed the thick emergency blanket Doc had packed, tossing it over the cat carrier. "Go to sleep, Foghorn."

"Foghorn Leghorn was a rooster," Cornelius started.

I held my fist in front of his face. "Don't make me pop you in the nose, Ghost Whisperer."

He stared at my fist, his cornflower blue eyes crossed. "You're bleeding, Violet."

Was I? I scowled at the wounds on the back of my hand. "That Chicken-saurus Rex has a mean pecker."

Harvey hooted. Before he could spit out whatever bawdy line that was hovering on the tip of his tongue, I leaned forward and tugged on his ear. "Zip it, ol' timer. Now give me one of those tissues in the glove box, please."

"Are you okay?" Doc asked, glancing in the mirror.

"Yeah." I took the tissue Harvey held out to me. "Elvis resisted arrest is all. The cat carrier must have reminded her of a previous cage she was stuffed into before Addy sprung her from the chicken farm."

I looked over Natalie's hands, but she seemed to be better at dodging Elvis's pecks than I was.

Something barked several times in succession in the front seat.

"What's that?" I asked.

"Coop's barkin' at me." Harvey pulled out his cell phone that was still sounding repeated "woofs" at him, ending any further chicken chatter. "What's shakin', Coop?" he answered the call.

I glanced at Natalie. She turned away and stared out the window, her jaw taut.

"Yep, we're skedaddlin' right now," Harvey told his nephew, then paused to listen. "No, I don't mean the royal 'we.' I mean me, Doc, Sparky, Corny, and Nat." Another pause. "I decided they needed my help, that's why." More silence from Harvey's end. "No, this has nothin' to do with yer mother's cookin', although her Christmas ham is always more like pork jerky. Makes my jaw ache to eat it." Harvey snorted at something Cooper said in reply to that, and then he frowned at Doc.

He held his phone away from his ear a moment later. "Coop says to tell ya that he just heard over the scanner there's a plow headin' up Strawberry. If ya can stick close to it, the driver is supposed to clear the road all of the way to the Rimrock Highway junction where there's a plow workin' that section down into Rapid."

"Got it," Doc said, his focus on the snow-covered road.

The sky was beginning to darken in the east. At the low speed we were forced to go, we'd be lucky to make it to the junction while it was still light out. Once the darkness took over for the night, it was going to be hell to see. Swirling snow in the headlights would force us to a crawl to be safe.

Harvey returned to the phone call. "Well, I'll give 'er a try, Coop, but ya know cell phones get sketchy out thatta way. With this snow, I reckon the signal will be scarce as gone." He nodded at whatever his nephew said. "Yeah. Keep an ear to the scanner. If anything happens, we'll flag down a plow."

A grunt or two later, Harvey hung up. "Coop says we're all two pickles short of a picnic fer tryin' to drive to Rapid in this mess, but he wishes us a Merry Christmas anyway."

Natalie sighed loud enough for my ears only. It sounded torn and heart-achy. I squeezed her leg, earning a shoulder bump and small smile in return.

We rolled past the hospital, one of the few places that would remain open for business besides the Deadwood police station. Everyone else could close up and head home to be with their families, taking the time to enjoy the buildup for the big day, watch holiday specials, and wrap those last-minute gifts. Images of my kids' smiling faces filtered through my thoughts, giving me a bright spot to focus on instead of Susan's sharp claws and menacing grin.

"Psychology," Cornelius said out of the blue.

"What about it?" I asked.

"That's what I majored in when I was in college."

"You have a degree in psychology?"

"No. I just majored in it." When I continued staring at him, he added, "I quit after my third year at the university."

"Why?" Natalie asked.

I wondered if it had anything to do with having enough family money that he didn't need to be concerned about a college degree or a career in the psychology field.

"My grandmother was growing weak with age. She told me that if I wanted to study under her and learn about being a soothsayer, I was running out of time. I decided that real-life experiences were far more important in my desired profession of paranormal studies and quit college, moving into her spare room."

"Did she teach ya about voodoo as well as bein' a seer?" Harvey asked.

"Voodoo and more. She was a patient and well-versed teacher. Christmas often reminds me of her."

"Why's that?" I asked. "Because you spent the holidays with her?"

"Because of mistletoe."

"What about it?"

"She kept bunches of it strung around her house year around."

"Why?"

"While mistletoe is a hemi-parasitical plant that can eventually kill its host tree, it has long been considered a good-luck plant. Hanging it throughout your house protects you from werewolves, as well as saving your children from being swapped with faerie changelings."

"And here I thought it was only good for kissing," Natalie joked.

Changelings, huh? I grimaced. Too bad the parents of the changeling ghost I agreed to help Cornelius trap didn't hang some mistletoe throughout their house.

He leaned back to look around me at Natalie. "Here's a bit of good news for ovulating females: The fresh juice from mistletoe berries increases fertility."

I cringed. Talk of babies often made my uterus run and hide under the nearest bed. Birthing and raising two kids on my own had sort of scarred me mentally as well as physically.

"You're scaring Violet's ovaries, Cornelius," Natalie said, grinning at my expression.

I glanced up and caught Doc glancing my way in the mirror. I made a cross with my fingers, warding him off. He chuckled and focused back on the road.

"Mistletoe also brings good luck," Cornelius told us.

"So did your grandmother have it hanging all over for good luck, or was it for protection from werewolves and changelings?" Natalie asked.

"In the voodoo religion," Cornelius explained, "mistletoe has other purposes such as keeping evil at bay and making love charms and sachet powders." Again, he leaned back and peered at Natalie. "Mixed with the right herbs, mistletoe is said to make a true-love powder."

"Really?" Harvey butted in, spinning partway around in his seat. "Do ya have the recipe fer this love potion?"

"Love powder," Cornelius clarified. "Yes, the recipe is somewhere in my grandmother's notes."

"Like you need that," I told the old goat. "You already have a harem of women at the senior center waiting for you to ask them to do some mattress dancing."

He snickered and turned back to the front. "Nothin' wrong with sprinklin' a little nookie guarantee into their prune juice, is there, stallion?" He nudged Doc with his elbow.

Doc shook his head, keeping his eyes on the road. He slowed to make the left turn onto US Highway 385.

"Here we go," I said under my breath.

Everyone quieted for a moment as we approached the bottom of Strawberry Hill. I waited until we were partway up to lean forward and touch Doc's shoulder. "How's it handling the snow?"

"Surefooted so far. Coop was right, though. The plow just went through, I can tell. But there are patches of ice that are only going to get worse."

I hunched my shoulders, feeling our escape window close. I crossed my fingers and toes, my gut knotting tighter with every mile we put between us and our warm, safe beds.

Doc leaned forward, both hands on the wheel as he rounded a corner with a steep dropoff on the passenger side into the ravine below. Even in the summer on dry pavement, some of the curves on Strawberry Hill had taken lives.

Natalie tugged my arm, pointing out her window. "Looks like the lanes coming down Strawberry haven't been cleared yet."

She was right. The other side of the road had several more inches of snow on it. I couldn't even see any tracks.

"In the past, when the snow comes down this hard and fast," Harvey explained, "the plows are stretched thin tryin' to keep up. The blade that we're followin' might be the one that's supposed to scrape back down into Deadwood."

Several minutes later, we all let out a breath of relief when Doc eased around the last precarious bend, ending our climb to flatter ground on top. While our journey through this shitstorm was far from over, the first hurdle was behind us.

I looked over my shoulder out the back window at the first dip of Strawberry Hill's steep, twisty slope into Deadwood. There was no turning back now. Going down that hill would be like a wild sled ride straight to Hell.

Chapter Seven

My struggles with sharing a planet with Susan probably could be traced back to my mom accidentally getting pregnant with another man's baby almost three years after I was born. The drunken one-night stand had happened during the six months or so when my parents were separated and on the verge of divorce, leaving my mom in a helluva situation until my dad stepped back into the picture and rescued her.

In spite of being adopted at birth by my dad and growing up under his roof, Susan was not my father's daughter—not physically, of course, but also mentally. They were night and day. The fact of her birth origin had remained unknown to Susan for decades, until I opened my big mouth in my twenties and spewed the truth about the family's secret in a flash of frenzied rage.

I still hung my head about that not-so-shining moment.

But back to Susan … It wasn't that I blamed my mom for Susan being one bubble off plumb. She and my father raised my sister with the same rules and values as those laid out for my brother, Quint, and me. My theory about the source of our constant clashing had more to do with mixing a good-for-nothing playboy's genes with my mother's flower-power DNA to produce a daughter who not only had a bulb or two burned out in her string of Christmas lights, but who also took great joy in smashing the pretty blinking bulbs in other people's strands.

Mainly mine.

Repeatedly.

My mother had spent one night in the arms of a man

who was totally opposite of my father both physically and mentally. Ironically, the spawn of that union had grown to be the bane of *my* existence, not my dad's.

Actually, now that I thought about it, Susan was only one of many banes for me. I seemed to be populating a village of them these days.

My cell phone rang, interrupting my trip to the past. A look at the screen made me sigh—the heavy, tired kind of sigh, not the lovesick sort that I usually did around Doc, who was currently aiming a raised brow my way in the rearview mirror.

"What do you need, Mom?" I answered, giving away the caller's identity in answer to Doc's questioning look.

Silence greeted me in return.

I checked the phone's screen. The call timer was still running. "Mom? Can you hear me?"

A hissing sound came through the line, followed by, "… she's worried you won't …" *hiss, crackle,* "… I can't calm her down …" silence, "… need to talk to her."

"What did you say, Mom? You cut out there for a bit. Who's worried about what?"

"Mommy, I miss …" silence, "… where are you? Layne doesn't think you …" *hissssss,* "… make it in time?" My daughter's voice came through broken up—due to both the lousy connection and her hitching sobs mixed between her words.

My throat tightened. "Baby, I'm on my way, I promise. Tell Layne we'll be there in plenty of time for Christmas." I crossed my fingers, shooting a worried glance at Natalie. She crossed her fingers, too.

"I'm afraid …" silence broken by a short *hiss,* "… need to hurry before …" *crackle,* "Santa comes."

"Don't worry, Addy. A little blizzard isn't going to keep Santa or me away."

"Mommy? I can't hear …"

Dead silence came through the line.

I checked the screen. The call timer had stopped. Shit. We'd been disconnected. Another look made my heart sink. Actually, it was worse than that. "Damn it. I have no service. Does anyone else have service right now?"

A quick group check found us all up shit creek.

"Criminy!" I dropped my phone in my lap. "That was Addy," I told Doc's reflection in the rearview mirror. "I think she's freaking out about the snow and us not making it down there for Christmas."

His forehead wrinkled. "We'll get there, Violet."

I rubbed the back of my neck, scowling at the flurries pelting the windshield. "I hope so," I whispered.

Natalie wound her arm around mine and shoulder bumped me. "Is Quint going to be home for Christmas?"

"Maybe." I leaned against the headrest. "Mom said he called last week from somewhere way north of the Canadian border and told her he was going to try to make it back in time, but he couldn't give any guarantees."

The world outside the windows looked straight out of the Great White North, so my brother would feel right at home. However, with the blizzard blowing in tonight and tomorrow, blanketing everything in thick snow, I doubted Quint would be able to make it if he wasn't already in town.

A short time later, we passed the road leading to Galena. Like Slagton, Galena had a few folks left rattling around in the old ghost town. However, unlike Slagton, Galena's remaining population contained normal people living among the historic buildings and graves, not odd whangdoodles who refused to heed the EPA's recommendation to leave due to contaminated water. However, I'd recently learned Slagton's remaining residents had a different reason for staying put besides pure orneriness—one that made me cringe even more.

I checked my cell phone again. Still no service. I blew

out a nervous breath, worrying my lower lip as I looked out one side of the vehicle and then the other. If we got stuck in the … No! I wasn't going to go there. I looked at my phone again. The no-service indicator held steady. I bounced my knees, my chest tightening as I stared at my cell phone, willing it to work.

Cornelius snatched my phone out of my hands.

"Hey," I said, reaching for it. "Give that back."

He tucked it inside his inner coat pocket, raising one black eyebrow. "Quint who?"

I reached for his coat opening, but he knocked my hand away. "Quint Parker, my brother."

"*You* have a brother?" His question held a fair amount of disbelief.

I thought he knew about my brother. "Is it so hard to imagine that I could share parents with a male representative of the human species?"

He cocked his head to the side, studying me. "What is the hair color of this male version of your parents' breeding?"

"Uh, dark."

A corner of his mouth twitched. "And his height?"

"As tall as the weeds in a widow's yard," I said, parroting my grandfather's description of Quint during his teen years.

"I see." Cornelius's gaze narrowed as he searched my face. "Based on your answers, I would hypothesize that his eyes are the same color as yours, his hair is wavy rather than curly, and he prefers to observe the world through the lens of a camera."

My jaw hit my knees. He'd nailed Quint, including his career as a photojournalist. "What is this? Some kind of mind-reading, voodoo trick? Did you learn how to do that when you weren't too busy training chimps to ride bicycles at the circus?"

"Unicycles, Violet. The monkeys rode only unicycles."
He scoffed. "The idea of a monkey riding a bicycle is simply
absurd. Such antics are better left to canines."

Natalie tried to smother a giggle and failed. I glanced at
her, thinking she was laughing at Cornelius's circus
comment, but then took a closer look. "Why are *you*
laughing, knucklehead?"

She shook her head, trying keep her lips pinched, but a
bubble of laughter slipped out.

When I turned back to Cornelius, his mouth twitched
again before he schooled his expression. "Okay, spill. How
do you know that about my …"

Then I remembered that when Cornelius was at our
family dinner a few weeks ago, he and Natalie had been
standing in front of the family photos on Aunt Zoe's wall.
One of the framed pictures was of Quint taken next to
some Native American ruins in New Mexico, wearing one
of his expensive cameras around his neck.

I squinted at him. "You're messing with me."

"I believe he's takin' yer mind off yer troubles," Harvey
piped up from the front seat. "That's a fine idea, bein's yer
sittin' there shakin' like a heifer with her first calf. Maybe we
should sing us some holiday tunes. I was always fond of
'Check the Balls on This Old Collie.' "

Doc's shoulders shook with laughter.

I crossed my arms. "That's not a real song."

"Is too. Want me to sing 'er fer ya?"

"One word, Harvey, and I'll sic Elvis and her
Tyrannosaurus pecker on you."

"Truth be told, Violet," Cornelius interjected, "I find it
interesting that you share your brother's eye color. It makes
me wonder what his view is on haints."

"What are haints?" Natalie asked.

"Ghosts," Doc answered. "The southern US variety."

Cornelius nodded. "My grandmother believed that a

channeler with light-colored eyes could see what she would call the 'choleric haints' easier than those with dark eyes."

"Choleric meaning sickly?" I asked.

"Bad-tempered," he clarified. "I think we can concur that you've seen a fair share of choleric haints during your channeling journeys."

A snort came from the ol' goat in the front passenger seat. "Sparky has a special skill when it comes to makin' folks puff up like a mad toad, whether they still breathe oxygen or not. Just ask Coop."

I pshawed. "Cooper chews up nails for breakfast each morning and spits out barbed wire come lunch. His opinion on my skills doesn't count." The dang detective woke up looking for trouble most days, especially when he came sniffing around me.

"What strikes me as odd," Cornelius continued, "is that you also appear to be able to touch, smell, and hear choleric haints, interacting with them in a way that is highly unusual compared to other channelers I've worked with in the past."

"I suspect Violet's abilities run deeper than our basic five senses," Doc spoke up on my behalf.

"You mean like a sixth sense?" Natalie asked.

"Deeper yet," he said, giving me a quick look in the rearview mirror.

Deeper how?

"Have you ever questioned your male sibling about his abilities to see in the dark?" Cornelius asked.

Cornelius's version of "the dark" was actually another realm full of not very nice beasties that reeked of hellish deeds and could see better than I could in the blackness. I shivered just thinking about my last visit to that dark world. Wouldn't Quint have mentioned something about the dark and its terrors if he knew about it?

"Or if this XY chromosome version of you has sensed

any other worldly presence during his travels?" Cornelius continued.

"No, but I'd think Quint would've mentioned it if he had."

"Would he, though?" Natalie bumped my knee with hers. "I mean, I know you two are close, but have you told him about your new career, Madame Executioner?"

I sputtered. "In my defense, that's not something that you just pick up the phone and blab about. It sort of needs to be shared face-to-face, and possibly with a good amount of liquor in hand."

I thought back to the night Doc and I had let Cooper in on our secret. The salty law dog had downed a couple of whiskeys after hearing the news, not liking the taste of what we were sharing one iota. It had taken him time to swallow that particular horse chestnut, prickly shell and all.

"So, if Quint shows up for Christmas, are you going to tell him?" Natalie pressed.

I pondered her question while staring out the windshield as we rolled past the road to Nemo, where Natalie's grandfather had a house. Since he'd married a widow from Arizona who owned an RV park down there, he hadn't spent much time in the hills.

"I don't know," was my final answer.

First, I doubted he'd believe me. Second, I hadn't a clue how to bring it up without sounding like a lunatic. Quint had always been pretty level-headed, not one to believe in ghosts even though he wore the protection charms Aunt Zoe made for him. "I'm not so sure telling Quint is a good idea. I mean, to what end? This is my problem, not his."

Natalie smirked. "Don't you think he might want to know that his sister is in mortal danger on a regular basis these days?"

"That would only worry him. Besides, it's not like he can stop the trouble yet to come. This killing gene only shows up in the females of our lineage."

"Yeah, but maybe he'll have a daughter some day."

I shook my head. "That would require Quint to settle down long enough to find a woman who will put up with his constant traveling, let alone be willing to have his kid. Currently, I don't see that happening. He's never had a girlfriend longer than a few months. I can't imagine him giving up the career he's worked so hard to build to stay put in one place anytime soon."

"That's true," Natalie said. "He's like Coop that way—career first, relationships second."

I ignored the bite in her tone. "But if Quint ever does have a daughter, I'll spill the beans." I'd have to for her protection in case she was forced to step up and face her demons, same as me. "That's if I'm still alive and kicking."

Doc's dark gaze met mine in the mirror. "You mean alive and *killing*, sweetheart."

"That, too."

"What about your other littermate?" Cornelius asked.

"Susan?" I grimaced. "I'm not sure Satan's concubine can even spawn humans from that stick insect body. Lord help us all if she makes mini versions of herself."

Natalie chuckled. "I can see the little devils running around your parents' place with their adorable tiny horns, sparking fires to everything they touch. Poor Grandma Hope will be singed from head to toe."

I grinned. "That's not much different from what Mom looks like after a weekend with my kids." I looked back at Cornelius. "Susan doesn't count when it comes to haints and the dark place."

"Violet's Executioner line is through her father," Doc explained. "Susan is not Blake's child, so she has no connection."

"She has no conscience, either," I grumbled.

"Ah." Cornelius stroked his goatee. "That explains why

you two have different smells."

I did a double take. "We smell different?"

"Invariably."

"What do I smell like?" The last individual who'd sniffed me told me I smelled like death, informing me that the lovely fragrance was something I came by naturally due to my lineage. Since then, I'd sniffed myself more times than I could count, worrying others could pick up the odor of death on me. I doubted that particular smell was anything close to the aroma of wildflowers I was aiming for with my lotions and perfume.

Cornelius shrugged. "You smell like Violet Parker."

I leaned forward. "Doc, you care to weigh in on this?"

Doc shrugged, too. "He's right. You smell like Violet."

"Is that bad?" Duh! How could the scent of death be good?

He glanced over his shoulder, flashing me a smolder-edged smile. "I find it incredibly intoxicating, Boots."

"Good answer." But I sat back, still frowning. I had a feeling Doc's nose didn't work when it came to me. Could Addy's pets smell a difference on me? Is that why Elvis had started leaving her eggs in Doc's shoes instead of mine lately? Why Bogart the cat kept bringing me other critters in bed?

Gah! I shook off my obsession with my smell and returned to what we'd been discussing before. "Susan is my mom's 'baby girl.' She's the end result of too much vodka during a lonely night when some good-looking tumbleweed blew into town." At least that was what my mom had explained to me in my twenties when I asked for details, curious who had replaced my father for a heartbeat or two in her past. "She's blind to my sister's atrocities." Whereas my mom examined my misdeeds painstakingly through a magnifying glass.

"Your mom isn't blind," Natalie said. "Hope sees the

best in everyone. It's one of her many delightful attributes."

Delightful? More like another reason to pull my hair out while in her company.

I pinched my lips together and looked out the windshield. Now was not the time to curl into a ball on the psychiatrist couch and share my emotional hang-ups when it came to my family. Christmas was enough at risk without my whining about growing up in a house with a vindictive sister who liked to burn my teddy bears.

We passed the road that led to Harvey's ranch and the town of Slagton several miles beyond. The wind was buffeting my SUV regularly now. The gusts whipped up swirls of snow in front of us, making it hard to see the road. Doc seemed to be taking our precarious sled ride in stride, the only evidence of his tension showing in his double grip on the steering wheel.

"What about your dad?" Doc asked, his gaze locked on the white mess out the windshield. "Is he aware of Susan's crimes against you?"

"Yeah, Dad knows what's going on. He always has. But when we were kids, he made sure we were punished accordingly, depending on who started the fight. Unfortunately, the instigator was usually Susan, and after a while she complained to one and all that he favored me over her. As the years passed, her anger at me for Dad's so-called bias spurred her into more destructive acts behind my parents' backs."

"Sounds like yer sister was rotten before she was even ripe," Harvey said.

"Exactly. The safest course for all of us this Christmas when it comes to Susan is—"

The sight of yellow and orange blinking lights ahead in the road made me pause. I leaned forward, squinting out the windshield. "What's that?"

Doc slowed as we neared the blinking lights.

"Why is the snowplow parked on the side of the road?" Natalie posed the question on all of our minds. "Please tell me he's taking a break to see a man about a mule and then he'll get back to work."

We stopped about twenty feet back from the big truck. The driver's door swung open and a pair of black snow boots appeared, followed by a burly bearded guy with a bright orange stocking hat and matching ski bib.

"I'm guessin' he's in a pickle," Harvey muttered.

Natalie cursed. "If he is, then we are, too."

The snowplow driver gave a come-here wave in our direction.

Doc opened his door. "I'll find out what's going on."

The four of us watched in silence as Doc and the snowplow driver conversed, their scene spotlighted by the headlights. After several slow nods, Doc looked back our way, his face drawn in a frown.

Harvey grunted. "That there look doesn't make me feel candy bar good."

My gut sank, too. I would've liked to have several candy bars at that moment, so I could shove them all in my mouth and wallow in chocolate until this damn snowy version of Hell went away.

The plow driver headed for his truck. Doc held up his index finger toward us, and then followed after the driver. He stood at the base of the steps leading up into the plow, looking up while the driver leaned inside the open cab.

"What do you think is going on?" I asked. "Are they shutting down the highway? Are we going to be stuck in the middle of nowhere in a blizzard for a week and end up on national news telling the world how we had to eat our leather gloves and boots to make it out alive?"

"Sheesh, Vi," Natalie said, groaning. "Why do you always think the worst first? Maybe they're just exchanging phone numbers so they can call each other sometime to meet for a beer."

I rolled my eyes so hard that my whole head turned along with them, ending up with my chin pointing in her direction. "Dear Lord! Is that the best you could come up with? Exchanging phone numbers in the middle of a freaking blizzard?"

"Violet's tendency toward negativity may have something to do with her DNA," Cornelius said, his focus still out the windshield. "Natural-born killers lean toward paranoia over positivity."

"I'm not negative," I said. "Or paranoid, either."

"Corny has a point," Harvey said. "Ya tend to think the boogeyman is out to get ya more often than not."

"That's because the boogeyman is out to get m—"

"Listen." Natalie held her hand up in my face, quieting me. She inched down her window. A high-pitched whining sound made us all look around through the windows in the back of the SUV.

The whining sound grew louder, coming closer. A snowmobile came into view through the swirling snow. He skirted my Honda and then pulled up next to where Doc was standing. Doc moved back as the snowplow driver stepped down into the snow, closing the plow door. After a handshake with Doc, the driver hopped on the back of the snowmobile and the machine spun around, zipping back past us without even a wave good-bye.

"What the hell?" Natalie mumbled, her face pressed against her window.

My heart pounded. "Uh, please tell me they are just taking a little break and are heading off to make snow angels where we can't watch."

Before anyone said anything else, Doc pulled open the door and slid inside. He turned in the seat and looked at me, his face grim. "I have good news and bad news. Which do you want first?"

"The good," Cornelius spoke up first. "My grandmother always said to choose positivity in the face of potential doom."

"Why's that?" Natalie asked.

"So you can die with a smile on your face."

I guffawed. "How is that better than being negative?"

Natalie covered my mouth. "Give us the good news, Doc."

"We have a full tank of gas."

Oh, crud. Was that the best he could offer? "That was a precaution on my part," I said, squashing his good news with reality. "Tell me the bad shit."

"The plow had a hydraulic line burst. That means the driver can't lower and raise the blade to adjust as he plows. There's no going forward until they get a mechanic out here to fix the hydraulic line."

I covered my eyes. "Oh, shit."

"Now do you want the real good news?" he asked.

I lowered my hand, glaring at him. "I'm going to hurt you when we make it to dry land."

He grinned. "The good news is we've been given orders to wait here."

"Here?" I gaped, looking out the window at the frozen wasteland around us.

"In the middle of god-forsaken-nowhere?" Natalie asked, finally hopping on my negativity bus.

Doc nodded. "We're to sit tight."

"Why?" Harvey asked. "Is San-ty Claus coming to rescue us?"

"Not this time. Your nephew heard about the hydraulic line bursting over the scanner. He left a message for us with the driver."

"What message?" Natalie asked.

"Coop is on his way." Doc looked beyond us out the back window. "And he's bringing the cavalry with him."

Chapter Eight

If time had taught me anything in this life, it was that too much of it spent with my sister always ended in a heartburning catastro-fuck, much like a volcanic eruption spewing poisonous, stinky gas and molten lava all over my family's get-togethers.

The burned heart in these explosions belonged to my mom, of course, since she usually blamed herself for the sub-surface tension that led up to the blast. My father often tried to protect Mom from the super-heated, pyroclastic flow once the shit started to fly, but a mere mortal could only work so much magic in the face of sheer doom.

My own beating organ had long ago developed a hard outer layer when it came to Susan, much like the Earth's crust. As long as I kept away from surefire hot spots, like all-inclusive multi-day family holidays, I remained fissure-free with all of my hot gas locked safely under the surface.

Susan was heartless. Therefore, she was unable to drum up any emotion from the deserted wasteland littered with jagged pieces of obsidian that was located between her lungs. While my parents disagreed with this diagnosis of my sister's internal landscape, I refused to re-evaluate the Bitch from Hell until I saw some sort of sign of life push up through the barren layers of ash.

This well-tested lesson about time and consequences brought me to one conclusion about my present situation: "I don't think I'm going to make it," I said aloud inside the crowded cab of my SUV, my voice strained.

Natalie pulled her nose from the window and the swirling white world beyond it. "Cripes, Vi. That registered around an eight-point-five on the doom-and-gloom scale."

"I'm reminded of an article I read about the Donner party's final lucid moments before they succumbed to cannibalism," Cornelius said.

I scowled at the leap he'd made between my despair and an urge to gnaw on another human. "If it comes to that, I'm eating you first, Cornelius."

"Sparky pro'ly needs to step outside and write her name in the snow," Harvey said from the front seat, his focus out the windshield. The wipers were starting to lose the battle against Mother Nature, struggling to keep the glass clear.

I followed his gaze, my eyes landing on the snowplow listing in the ditch in front of us like a battered ship. It blinked methodically in the waning light, beached in a sea of white swells. Maybe I should go jump off its helm.

"Violet." Doc stared at me in the rearview mirror. "You know that going outside right now is a bad idea."

How did he know I'd been pondering diving headfirst into a snow bank?

Harvey shifted, glancing Doc's way. "Maybe so, but it'd sure make my bladder gladder if I went out there. Hell, my inkwell is 'bout to start leakin', too."

"I don't need to use the restroom," I told my fellow lifeboat members.

"What did you mean then about not making it?" Natalie asked, her eyes searching my face. "You're not going to start flipping out, are you? Because now is not a good time to start foaming at the mouth." She wrinkled her nose. "You'll get me all wet."

"I'm not going to flip out."

A squawk came from the back of the vehicle.

My left eye twitched at the sound of Addy's dang bird. Twice. I looked away, trying to hide the telltale sign of my fissures widening on the inside.

"I saw that," she said, pointing at my face. "You're

starting to twitch. Doc, you need to calm her down."

I glared at her finger. "What is Doc supposed to do?"

"I don't know, kiss you senseless to take your mind off the current situation."

I guffawed. "Come on, Doc's good, but it's going to take more than a kiss to make me forget that we're stuck out here in the middle of nowhere in a stupid freaking blizzard and it's all my fault because none of you would be here with me, risking your lives, if I hadn't put my career before my children." That last bit came out as a croak due to running out of air.

Silence filled the cab, all eyes on me.

"No offense, Doc," I whispered, blinking back a swell of guilt and anger and frustration all condensed in a couple of stupid tears.

"None taken, Boots." He twisted in his seat and took my clasped hands in his. "I'd rather be here with you in the middle of this storm than anywhere else right now."

I blinked several more times. It was no wonder my heart sighed like a lovesick skunk whenever he was near. "Stop being nice to me when you should be telling me that I was an idiot to pooh-pooh the storm predictions."

Harvey snorted. "This is a bunch of turkey hooves."

I recoiled. "What?"

"This whimperin' business of yers is a bushel full of nonsense. We're here by choice. If we didn't wanna come, we'd have dug in our heels and stayed put down in Deadwood."

"Yeah, but if I'd left yesterday with the kids instead of waiting until this afternoon—"

"Then Harvey, Corny, and I would all be alone for Christmas," Natalie finished. "Instead, we're lucky enough to be hanging out in this cozy cab with you."

Another squawk came from the back seat, louder this time, followed by several indignant-sounding clucks.

Natalie chuckled. "Elvis is glad, too. She would've been stuck in the basement for days if it wasn't for you."

I looked back at Doc, whose hand still held mine. "But what if we're stuck here all night?"

"Coop's coming," Natalie said, growling something under her breath that sounded like *damn it*.

"But what if he doesn't make it?"

"He'll make it," Doc assured me, squeezing my hands once more before letting them go.

"What makes you all so certain?"

Harvey pointed in Natalie's direction. "Coop's sufferin' from Cupid's cramps, and we got his cure-all sittin' here with us. He ain't gonna let anything happen to her or the rest of us, fer that matter. If he says he's comin', ya can count on him like warts on a toad."

Natalie's gaze tightened. "I told you before, there's nothing going on between Coop and me."

He hooted back at her. "Well, then someone better tell yer eyeballs that, 'cause they get big and googly when Coop steps into the room."

She gasped. "They do not, you ornery blowhard."

My eye twitched again. Ignoring their bickering, I nudged Cornelius's arm. "I need you to take my mind off our current predicament. You know, like you did when you took my phone."

He stared out his window. "No, thank you. I'm fine."

Wait. What? I leaned closer to him. "What do you mean, 'No, thank you'?"

"You're not my type, Violet."

Not his … I shook my head, feeling like I'd missed something. "What are you talking about?"

He spared me a glance. "I'm not into blondes."

My jaw tightened. "What do you have against blondes?"

"Studies have shown brunettes have stronger immune systems and are, therefore, less susceptible to diseases and stress." He jabbed his thumb in Natalie's direction. "Case in point—that brunette is playful and relaxed while your escalating stress level is making your eye twitch."

I covered my twitching eye, looking over at Natalie's flared nostrils and red cheeks and then back at Cornelius. "You call that playful? If Harvey doesn't quit picking on her about Cooper, she's going to wallop him with her hammer."

"I'd call that spirited. Brunette members of the female species are known to be more emotional, whereas blondes are often described as heartless and icy."

I glared at him with my non-twitching eye. "We are not icy. Blondes are hot tempered just like brunettes and redheads, aren't we, Doc?" My gaze swung to the front seat.

Doc raised both hands. "You'll get no argument from me, Killer."

"See," I said, my focus back on Cornelius.

"The Tall Medium's opinion is invalid in this case."

"Why?"

"Because you exchange bodily fluids with him, and he's intelligent enough to realize that agreeing with you will allow him to continue participating in rhythmic coitus with you."

Doc chuckled. "I do enjoy a good romp of rhythmic coitus with a hot-tempered, blond Executioner when the opportunity arises."

"What's this here now about someone havin' coitus?" Harvey asked, butting into our conversation.

I ignored Harvey's gold-toothed grin. "If you aren't into blondes," I said to Cornelius, "then why were you drooling over that clockmaker?"

He shrugged. "She's not a blonde."

"What is she then?"

"Otherworldly."

He had a point there.

"And her lips glowed," he added.

"Which lips?" Harvey asked.

After aiming a scowl in the dirty old bird's direction, I told Cornelius, "Her lips did not glow." Although the rest of her seemed to emit some sort of radiant light.

"I'm not going to kiss you, Violet," Cornelius said.

I stammered. "K-k-kiss me?" I glanced at Doc, who was watching our play-by-play with a grin on his face, darn him.

Cornelius studied his long bony fingers, as if we were discussing his last manicure. "Besides your hair color being a problem for me, sharing a single kiss can transfer up to a million bacteria, and I'm not interested in accumulating the bacteria from someone of your breeding."

My breeding?

A cackle-like sound came from the feather-covered peanut gallery in the cat carrier behind me.

I poked him in the leg. "First of all, I didn't ask you to kiss me, Cornelius. Second, don't you dare ruin kissing for me with a bunch of gross facts."

Harvey snickered. "I once read in one of those ladies' magazines that kissin' is good fer ya. It makes ya extra slobbery, which helps to prevent yer teeth from rottin' out of yer head."

Natalie leaned over, joining in. "I read something about how kissing can lower stress and blood pressure." She elbowed me. "You could use that in spades about now. Maybe I should switch places with Doc so we can test that."

"Doc and I are not going to sit here and have a makeout session in front of you three to see if it will lower my blood pressure."

"Why not?" Harvey asked. "We're packed in here like cows in a haulin' trailer with nothin' else to do while we wait fer Coop to ride in on a red-nosed reindeer."

I frowned at Doc. "You're not helping me here."

He winked at me. "You lost me at rhythmic coitus."

"Over ninety percent of women like to be kissed on the

neck," Cornelius pontificated, still on his factoid kick.

Harvey looked at Doc. "Does Sparky like it on the neck or somewhere else better?"

Doc mimed zipping his lips.

Smart man.

"Where I like to be kissed is nobody's business but Doc's and mine."

"According to one of my college textbooks," Cornelius said, lacing his fingers in his lap, "psychopaths are more likely to kiss with their eyes open."

"How do you remember all of this nutty stuff?" I asked.

"I like to read."

"Does Sparky kiss with 'er eyes open?" Harvey badgered Doc.

"I once dated a guy who kept his eyes open when we made out," Natalie said. "It messed with my head. You know, knocked me off my game. It was like kissing Igor from that movie *Young Frankenstein*, because his eyes started going all wobbly when he got hot and bothered."

"You dated a guy with eyes like Marty Feldman's?" Doc asked, breaking his silence.

She nodded. "He had an incredible body to make up for them. Remember that time we saw him naked, Vi?"

Doc raised his brow. "Naked, huh?"

"I don't know what she's talking about," I fibbed. "She must be getting cabin fever."

"But I ended up breaking up with him before we ever made it into the bedroom because I kept singing, 'Jeepers creepers, where'd you get those peepers' in my head whenever he kissed me. Made me giggle when I was supposed to be sighing and moaning."

Elvis let out a series of loud squawks that made me nearly jump out of my skin. "What is wrong with that stupid bird?"

A fluttering sound came from the cat carrier, followed

by more squawks.

"Maybe she wants to write her name in the snow, like me," Harvey said. "After being cooped up in this sardine can fer so long, maybe the bird just wants to stick 'er pecker out in the fresh air."

Natalie smiled. "Are we talking about the bird or you?"

"Yep." Harvey shoved open his door. "I'll be back in two shakes."

After the door closed, I asked Doc, "Should Harvey go out there alone?"

One of his dark brows inched upward. "You want me to go hold his hand?"

"Maybe, smartass."

Doc gazed out the passenger side window. "He's not going too far." I started to follow his gaze, but he blocked my view with his hand. "You don't want to see this. I think he's writing in cursive."

I cringed and then took his hand, kissing his knuckles, before handing it back.

He frowned down at his hand. "Now I have your bacteria all over me."

I blew him a kiss, but then sobered. "I'm sorry I made you drive us out here."

"Violet, quit taking ownership of this situation. You have no more control over the weather or that plow's broken hydraulic line than you do Addy's chicken."

Elvis let out a series of cackle-squawks, as if on cue.

"I just wanted your first Christmas with me to be filled with family fun stuff—the good kind of family, not my sister and her diabolical crap."

He opened his mouth to reply, but Elvis started flapping around again, making ear-piercing noises along with loud thumps inside the carrier.

"What in the hell is wrong with that chicken?" Natalie said, turning around in her seat. She pulled off the blanket that I'd used to cover the cat crate, sending tiny feathers floating through the cab.

The squawking grew even louder, followed by thumping and clanging as Elvis tried to escape the carrier through the closed cage door.

"Let me out," I said, nudging her leg.

"What are you going to do?" Doc asked.

"Calm her down somehow before she breaks a wing."

Natalie frowned at me. "What do you think you are, a chicken whisperer?"

"Maybe. Open the damned door, mother clucker."

"Okay, okay." She spun back around and opened the door, wrapping her scarf tighter around her neck as she stepped out into the snow and wind.

Before following her, I looked back at Cornelius. "Thank you, by the way."

"For what?"

"Distracting me again."

His crooked smile made a brief appearance. "I don't know what you're talking about, Violet."

I joined Natalie, my boots sinking a couple of inches into the snow piling up in the plow's wake. The freezing wind cut through my wool coat like it was peppered with holes.

Doc joined us, pulling on his gloves. "Come on."

The three of us made our way around the back of the SUV, hunched partway over to stave off the breath-stealing wind that tore at our coats and pelted us with snow. Doc opened the back door and dragged the cat carrier to the edge of the bumper.

I squatted and peered into the carrier. Elvis was still fluttering and flapping in the tight space. I thought I saw a streak of something dark on her white feathers. My heart tightened. Was that blood? Shit! If anything happened to the crazy bird, Addy would never forgive me.

"What should we do?" Natalie hollered over the wind.

"Addy told me once that she thinks Elvis is claustrophobic. Maybe if I let her out in the back end for a little bit, she'll calm down."

"Claustrophobic?" Doc repeated. "That doesn't make any sense. Elvis likes to roost in small spaces, like your closet."

That was true. I tried to hold the cat carrier still as the bird jostled around inside, willing her to chill out. "Well then," I told him, "maybe she needs to go see a man about a mule."

He stared at me for several beats, and then let out a loud laugh.

"I'm serious. Addy has her potty trained. Maybe she doesn't want to pee in the cat carrier."

Natalie bumped my arm. "Did you bring her leash?"

"I thought I told you to grab it."

"No, you told me to get Elvis's favorite sweater. The one your mom made with the poodle on it."

"Crap. I forgot the leash." The carrier shook in my hands as Elvis went ape-shit again. "If I let her go, you think she'll stick around?"

"Where's she going to go in this storm?" Natalie yelled. "Out for an evening stroll to try and pick up a rooster or two?"

"Maybe she'll cross the road," I snapped back, pointing at the trees lining the ditch over there. I could barely see the pines through the snow whipping and churning around us.

Doc laughed again. "Do you hear yourself?"

I swatted his chest and then leaned down and popped open the cage door, reaching inside to grab the silly bird. Something pinched the webbing between my thumb and index finger through my glove.

"Ouch!" I yelled, yanking my hand back. My glove caught on the cage door, pulling the carrier with it. The cage slid forward and landed upside down on the snow.

"Son of a peach!" I yelled.

Doc bent down to scoop it up, but Elvis made her escape before he got it back topside. Natalie reached for the bird, but she shot off across the snowy ditch, running toward the trees like a jailbird who'd scaled the prison wall.

"Elvis, no!" I yelled, starting after her.

Doc caught my arm and dragged anchor.

"Doc, let go! I have to—"

"Violet," he hollered above the storm. "You are not following that chicken into the trees and getting lost in this blizzard!"

I frowned after the bird, trying to see her white tail feathers through the whirling snow. My heart pounded in my ears, blocking out the whistling wind.

Hell's bells.

Elvis was gone.

"Fuck!"

Chapter Nine

US Highway 385, twenty-one miles out of Deadwood
7:35 p.m.

It was going to be a blue, blue Christmas without Elvis. Crud.

I could avoid telling Addy that her chicken had run away in the middle of a snowstorm and most likely frozen her tail feathers off. That would delay the aftermath of tears for the time being, but the truth would come out as soon as we returned home to a chicken-less basement.

Damn. There'd be no end to the buckets of drama and hours of blame-laced wails.

I buried my face in my gloves. It'd be like reliving Christmas break back when fifteen-year-old Susan stole my driver's license and Mom's car keys, snuck out after midnight, and got busted by the cops as she was spinning doughnuts in the school parking lot with a car full of her friends all sloshed on peppermint schnapps.

Susan's drunken accusations later that night about how her illicit actions were all *my* fault because I'd refused to sneak her over to her friend's party had turned my mom into a fire-breathing dragon. Quint had been on a photography field trip to the Everglades for college credits that year, so he'd lucked out, dodging the ear-ringing fireworks.

Good ol' Susan. She was such a pro at pissing all over our happy family moments. Just once I'd like to … Never mind. This was not the time to reminisce about Susan's history of wreaking holiday havoc. I had a bigger problem at the moment. Bigger even than a missing chicken.

I lowered my hands and staggered around to the front of my rig, leaning into the blasts of cold air.

"Winter wonderland, my ass," I bellyached, my teeth chattering while the frigid wind rocked me in my boots. Snow pelted my face, sticking to my eyelashes.

I shivered, my shoulders pulling in tight as I stood in the middle of the two-lane highway. My SUV's headlights blazed from behind me, but in a storm this fierce, the bright beams of light weren't much help. They reflected off the swirling flakes, blinding me rather than illuminating the vast stretch of dark, empty snow-covered road in front of me.

Old Man Winter could be such a dick. He'd gone and coated the hills in a thick blanket of white on Christmas Eve of all days. It was going to take at least a week of December sunshine to melt this white fluffy crap away. I scowled long and hard, not giving a flying reindeer if my face froze that way either.

The wind raged and howled around me, tearing through my blue wool coat. It stole my breath and gripped my bones with its freezing fingers. I tucked my scarf tighter around me, weighing my options. The blizzard had crowded into the Black Hills so fast, pushing and shoving to make it in time for Christmas.

Trudging ahead through the frozen tundra would be right up there with dodging icebergs in the North Atlantic. Besides, my new purple snow boots were no match for the drifts, many of which were already knee-deep and rising.

"Razzle-frazzit," I muttered through stiff lips.

Down on the prairie in the warm bosom of my parents' house, my two kids were waiting for Santa and me to show. Earlier on the phone, I'd reassured them the snowy roads wouldn't stop me from arriving in time to help them prep for St. Nick. Little had I realized then that Old Man Winter had a plan to knock me on my caboose and then kick me while I was down.

But I wasn't waving any white flags yet. Nope. I still had plenty of grit in my gizzard. Raising my gloved hands, I aimed both middle fingers at the sky. "Kiss off, icehole!"

A strong gust of wind rammed me from behind, knocking me to my hands and knees in the snow. Cold wetness soaked through my jeans and gloves. Before I could catch my breath, another blast of air hit me, blowing snow into my face.

Son of a sugarplum!

I wiped at my eyes with my coat sleeve. Rolling onto my back, I stared up at the maelstrom whirling overhead. Somehow, I had to make it to my kids through this frozen wasteland.

The only thing left to do at this point was wait for Cooper and his so-called cavalry. Although unless he had a sleigh and eight flying reindeer, I wasn't sure how he could help me get home for Christmas—chicken or no chicken.

The purr of my Honda's engine held a steady rhythm under the moaning and whistling wind, reminding me of one of those nature relaxation soundtracks. Unfortunately, it did nothing to help lower my blood pressure.

Poor Addy. This holiday was going to be so hard on her. How was I going to make up for losing Elvis?

A squall of snow swirled over me, dusting me from head to toe. I closed my eyes and mopped my face, the stinging cold no match for the anxiety pinching my chest.

One thing I could try to do to make Christmas better for everyone *if* we made it to my parents' place was not fight with Susan. As much as the thought of putting up with my sister's conniving bullshit made me grind my molars, the next couple of days would be much merrier if I didn't let her goad me into another bicker-fest.

Although, if that jezebel laid one finger on …

Cluck.

I blinked open my snow-coated lashes. A white chicken head filled my vision, the red comb sprinkled with snowflakes.

Cluck cluck. Elvis flutter-hopped onto my chest. She stared down at me, turning her head in jerky movements one way and then the other. *Cluck.*

"Elvis! You came back to me." I hugged her to my chest until she squawked and pecked at my gloved knuckles. "My sweet little good-luck charm."

"Violet?" Doc kneeled in the snow next to me, the headlights spotlighting his profile. "What are you doing down here?" He plucked a feather from my hat. "Did you slip and fall?"

"I'm just chillin' with my peep." I nuzzled Elvis again.

A grin split the half of his face that was visible in the light. He glanced up at Natalie, who'd joined our little reunion. "I think she's officially starting to unravel."

She guffawed. "She's been unraveling since she played hide and seek in the creepy Hessler house last summer. All of that clown shit scrambled her egg."

Cornelius came up next to Natalie and looked down at me with a perplexed expression. "Did you know that a group of clowns is called a 'clown alley'?"

I shuddered at the thought of running into even a single clown in an alley. Natalie was right, that night in the Hessler house had cracked my noggin and shaken up my world.

"Hey, when did Sparky lose 'er vertical hold?" Harvey hollered, leaning into the wind by my knees.

"I once dated a guy who was a rodeo clown," Natalie told Cornelius. "His stage name was Horn E. Butt."

I groaned, remembering Horn and his collection of raunchy belt buckles and frequent rude gestures.

"Did he live up to his name?" Harvey asked.

She scowled. "I guess. He was already sleeping with three other women when we started dating. One turned out to be his wife, who claimed eight seconds was about all Horn was good for most nights."

The rumbling sound underneath the wind deepened, growing louder.

"Do you guys hear that?" I handed Doc the chicken and sat up. "We should put a sweater on that bird before she gets freezer burn."

"Or a bathing suit."

I did a double take. "Why a bathing suit?"

"The best way to quickly defrost a frozen chicken is in a cold water bath," Doc said matter-of-factly.

I grinned. "Funny and sexy. I'm a lucky girl."

He winked, leaning closer. "Don't forget 'good for more than eight seconds,' too."

"Most of the time, Candy Cane," I teased and kissed his cold lips.

He laughed and passed Elvis to Natalie, and then he held out his hand to help me up. "Do we hear what, Killer?" he asked while helping me brush off my backside rather thoroughly.

"That rumbling." I adjusted my hat so it didn't cover my ears, listening in the wind. The sound was definitely louder, sort of growling now. "I think it's coming from that way." I pointed toward the dark road behind us.

Natalie moved up next to me, Elvis wrapped in her arms, and stared into the darkness behind my Honda. "Maybe the snowplow driver is coming back with a mechanic."

"That ain't no whiny snowmobile engine," Harvey said, walking past us. He stopped at the back bumper and stared into the flying snow beyond it.

We all joined him, Natalie pausing long enough to shove Elvis inside the warm vehicle.

What started as a dull glow in the darkness grew and brightened as the rumbling intensified.

"It sounds like my uncle's Sherman tank," Cornelius said next to me.

Harvey did a double-take. "Yer uncle has a tank?"

"He has three, including a Panzer. He takes his war games seriously."

Harvey's two gold teeth glittered in the red glow of my taillights. "I'd sure like to play on his battlefield."

"You think that's Cooper and his cavalry?" I asked nobody in particular.

"I sure hope so," Harvey sniffed. " 'Cause it's cold as a cast-iron commode out here, and my twig and berries are one stiff breeze from breakin' free and blowin' clear to the Wyoming state line."

"Mine, too," Natalie said, shivering. When Harvey and I both frowned at her, she added, "My berries, I mean, since I'm currently twig-less due to my sabbatical."

"You're twig-less, all right," I said.

"Can it, ninnyhammer." She nudged me into Doc, who steadied me in front of him.

The glow became a glare in the white landscape, making me squint. I counted eight headlamps. "What is it?" I asked Doc as the engine growl became louder than the wind.

"A snowcat."

I shielded my eyes as the imposing beast of a machine came to a stop in front of us. "Where on earth did Cooper get a snowcat on Christmas Eve?" I shouted above the noise.

Harvey grabbed my elbow and tugged me off to the right, out of the bright spotlights. The diesel engine idled down to a low, rhythmic rattle, making it easier to hear. "It ain't Coop's, it's Reid's."

Now that I wasn't blinded by the eight headlamps, I had a better view of the snowcat. Sporting a snow blade on the front and two wide tracks in place of wheels, the big boxy cab had four windows running along each side and a rack on the top.

The driver-side door opened. Reid Martin crawled out onto the wide track and jumped down to the road, joining us along with Doc.

Reid's red canvas coat and Santa hat matched the color of his snowcat. "Hey, Sparky. I hear you're in need of a big strong fireman again."

I laughed and gave him a hug. He smelled like hot chocolate and felt as warm as a toasted marshmallow. "Am I glad to see you, Fire Captain Martin. Please tell me you left a certain crabby-pants elf back in Deadwood."

"Nope. Coop threatened me with bodily harm if I didn't bring him along for the ride. He's inside letting dispatch know we found you."

Dang. Of course Cooper would want to come up here and chew me out in person for dragging his uncle into this blustering mess.

"What do you have there, Martin?" Doc asked, pointing at the snowcat. "A magic sleigh?"

Reid grinned, thumbing toward the snowcat. "That little thing? That's a '74 Thiokol Spryte 1200C with 44-inch wide tracks able to cut through sand, swamp, mud, snow, or anything else you can throw in its path."

"Like this blizzard?" I asked.

His eyes crinkled in the corners. "Sure. I can punch a road through the snow without breaking a sweat and haul your gear up top, too."

Doc's face lit up as he admired Reid's big-boy toy. "Where'd you pick that up?"

"Yellowstone National Park was auctioning off its old snowcats a few years back. I grabbed one, figuring it'd be good to have here in the hills for emergencies in the backcountry. I gutted the back and refitted it with fold-up bench seats in case I needed to use it as a makeshift ambulance."

I joined Doc in his admiration. Something this big could fit all of us in it and my Christmas haul, too. "How fast does it go, Reid?"

"Fast enough to get you down to Rapid City in time for Santa Claus to wiggle down that chimney."

Cooper rounded the front of the snowcat. "Dotty wanted me to remind you that you're invited to her place for Christmas dinner if you have nowhere else to go," he told Reid, before turning on me with a chiseled glare under his black knit beanie hat. He crossed his arms, looking even bigger and more intimidating than usual in his bulky police coat. "Parker, you picked one hell of a night to get stuck out in the middle of nowhere."

I raised my chin. "Did you come all of the way up here to rub that in, Cooper?"

"No. I came up here to drag your ass back to town."

I dug in my heels. "I'm not going back to Deadwood."

"Yes, you are."

"No, she's not." Natalie took my side, literally, and locked elbows with me. "And you can't make us."

Cooper's gaze narrowed as he looked back and forth between us.

"We're headin' down to Rapid, Coop," Harvey said, huddling his shoulders as a stiff wind rattled us. "And yer comin', too."

"Why would I do that?"

"Because we want you to," I said, bumping Natalie's shoulder. "Don't we, Nat?"

"Yeah, we sure do," Natalie said, although she could have tried harder to sound like she meant it, darn it.

I turned to Reid. "You have enough fuel to get us down to Rapid?"

He nodded. "But I need a favor in return."

"Name it."

"Invite me to stay for Christmas. I have something I

want to give Zo."

"Martin," Cooper butted in. "This was not part of the plan that we talked about on the way up here."

"Not what you planned, maybe," Reid said with a twinkle in his eye. "But I had something else in mind when I agreed to go for a ride in the snow."

Cooper cursed. "What makes you think Zoe won't chase you away with her shotgun again when you show up on her brother's doorstep?"

"For one thing," Reid said, "I'm betting she left her shotgun at home."

"Fer another," Harvey added, "he's savin' the day by haulin' us all down out of the harrowin' cold and snow to safety." He patted Reid's shoulder. "That there oughta win ya a kiss under the mistletoe from the hard-headed woman."

"Maybe even two," I said, feeling lighter than I had since the snow started falling hours ago in Deadwood. I looked over at Cornelius, who was already untying the trident from the top of my rig, while Elvis walked back and forth along the top of the back seat inside.

"What do you say, Reid?" I spread my arms wide. "Would you like to join us for Christmas down at my parents' place?" I asked officially. "You can bring a guest if you'd like, but he has to promise not to arrest anyone while he's there."

Reid's laughter was swallowed by the wind. "I'd love to come to your family Christmas, Sparky. Thanks for asking."

I turned to Cooper. "Well, Detective? You think you can stomach a bit of family excitement without pulling out your handcuffs?"

"I left my handcuffs back at Nyce's place," he said, looking at Natalie for a moment before giving in with a nod. "Fine, Parker. Let's get the hell out of here before I end up stuck in that damned snowcat with you for the night."

"That's the Christmas spirit, Coop," I said with a chuckle and gave him a playful punch in the shoulder.

"That's 'Cooper' to you, Parker," he said and joined Doc and Reid in unloading my SUV.

Natalie watched him walk away. "Well, so much for my relaxing Christmas with your family."

I scoffed. "Like that was even going to happen with Susan in the picture."

Harvey chortled next to me. "Yer aunt's in fer a big Christmas surprise, Sparky."

He was spot on there. Aunt Zoe was going to pop a gasket when she saw Reid walk in with us, but if I could be nice to Susan, she could play nice with her ex.

I pulled my hat down lower. "Just keep your fingers crossed this whole holiday doesn't blow up in our faces."

Chapter Ten

One Hour Until Christmas …

By the time we rumbled into Rapid City, Old Man Winter had covered the prairie in almost a foot of snow. Judging by the thick flurries still coming down, he didn't look to be taking a break anytime soon.

I texted Aunt Zoe as soon as I had cell service. I couldn't spring Reid on her without a little warning, but I decided the best course of action was to ease into it: *Please tell me Susan went out for milk, got lost in the storm, and won't be there when I arrive.*

You're not that lucky, Aunt Zoe replied within seconds. *Where are you?*

Almost there. I glanced up at Reid and winced. Inviting him along was going to win me a night in the doghouse.

How long until you get here?

Maybe ten minutes. How's Dad?

With any luck, my father would be sleeping when we arrived and not tackle Reid on the front lawn.

There was a slight pause, and then she replied with: *Your father is fine. What's going on?*

Nothing.

I'm sure your nose is twitching, baby girl. Cough it up.

I hesitated, looking around at my fellow passengers in turn. Harvey had sprawled out on the bench next to me, snoozing as we bounced along. How he could sleep through the growling engine and periodic lurches was beyond me. Cornelius and Natalie were sitting on the bench across the cab where he was teaching her an old Japanese version of rock-paper-scissors that used a frog, a slug, and a snake instead. The Japanese game's hand signs were different enough that it had taken Natalie half of the ride and plenty of laughs to get used to them. Up front, Doc was keeping Reid and Cooper company, sitting behind the center console on an army-style footlocker Reid used to store his tools. That left Elvis, who was sleeping in the cat carrier with the cage door open in case she needed to stretch her legs.

Short of singing Christmas carols, a suggestion by Harvey that Cooper shot down in a flash—as in he flashed his Colt .45 and threatened to put a bullet in the ass of the first one to burst into song—we were one jingly song short of a fun sleigh ride while dashing through the snow.

Unfortunately, the relaxed atmosphere inside the cozy cab had a short shelf life. I peered out through the snow-lined window. Very short, actually, as in my parents' street was less than three miles away.

The trip down the hills had taken longer than Reid had predicted. This blizzard had been one hell of an opponent from the get-go.

After plowing a path through the snow to a nearby side road where I could safely leave my SUV, Reid had ushered us into the snowcat and started the trek through the winter wonderland. He'd been forced to take it slow on the way down out of the hills due to periodic whiteouts making it impossible to see. In a few places, he'd lowered his plow to break through drifts that were stacked up too high for safe passage. Several times, when he couldn't see the markers lining the sides of bridges and cliff edges, we'd had to stop while Doc and Cooper took turns climbing out to clear snow off the front of the snowcat. But not once throughout the whole white-knuckle ordeal had Reid complained about having to come out in this blizzard to save us.

However, while Reid had remained cool, calm, and

grinning through it all, I'd been a hot mess. Half of the time I was wringing my hands about the snowcat breaking down and leaving us stranded in the middle of nowhere with nothing left to eat but Elvis the chicken. The rest of the time I was sweating inside and out about how mad Aunt Zoe and my dad were going to be when they found out I'd invited Reid to Christmas.

Now that we'd made it safely down to the prairie, I was beginning to think eating Elvis might have been the better of the two endings.

You still there? Aunt Zoe texted.

I need a favor, I wrote back.

What?

Get Dad drunk really quick.

Why?

I'm not alone.

I know. Your mother told me that Nat, Cornelius, and Willis are tagging along with Doc and you.

Cringing, I typed: *There are more.*

This time Aunt Zoe took longer to reply. Then one word popped up on my screen in all caps: *WHO?*

Cooper and one other.

Please tell me Reid Martin is not about to land on my doorstep.

Well, technically, it's not YOUR doorstep. Her doorstep was in Deadwood buried under several feet of snow by now.

VIOLET LYNN!

Okay, okay. Reid is with us.

Explain.

The snowplow we were following broke down.

What's that have to do with Reid?

I'll tell you in about three minutes.

It turned out to be more like five because Reid dropped into a lower gear once we turned into my parents' neighborhood so the rumbling engine wouldn't wake up those little ones already dreaming of Santa and his reindeer.

Aunt Zoe was standing alone on the front porch when Reid rolled in behind her pickup and cut the engine. She wore my dad's black puffy coat and a scowl reminiscent of the Grinch. Her long silver-streaked hair was plaited in a braid that draped down over her shoulder.

"Uh-oh," Reid said in the sudden silence. "That's not a happy-to-see-me face."

Harvey sat up and peered out the window. "Zoe's got 'er horns out already. Sparky must have spilled the beans about you joinin' the roundup."

"Guilty." I pocketed my phone. "I wanted her to run interference with Dad. We don't need a replay of our last family get-together. One barroom brawl played out in the front yard is enough for one month."

Cooper frowned at Reid and then me. "I told you two this was a bad idea."

"Yeah, yeah," Reid said. "I know it's a long shot with a limb in the way, but I have to try. Zo's worth it."

Harvey grunted. "Where do ya figure we can shuck our boots and stretch out for the night?"

"Doc and Vi will stay at her parents'." Natalie pulled a key ring from her pocket and jingled the keys. "The rest of us can sleep next door at my aunt Deborah's place. I'm taking care of her house while she's down in Arizona. It has four bedrooms with beds in each, so we just need to throw on the sheets and blankets."

"There are five of us," Cooper pointed out, his gaze holding steady on Natalie.

"Nat can share a bunk with me," Harvey said.

Cooper's eyes moved to his uncle. "Why you?"

"Well, we both tend to saw logs in our sleep fer one thing." Harvey grinned wide. "And I know I can keep my hands to myself all night long."

Both Natalie and Cooper looked away, no argument from either on that score.

"Zo's waving us in," Reid said and pushed open his door. "Might as well go see if she's in a swinging mood tonight. Anybody bring any mistletoe along?"

Cooper cursed and grumbled before following Reid's lead.

"Coop must've forgotten his Christmas spirit back in Deadwood," Doc said to me.

I chuckled. "I suspect he filled it full of bullet holes and buried it out back of Harvey's ranch for the dog to find."

"Yup. Ol' Red will dig 'er up in the spring and leave it on my doormat, same as he has with all the other pieces and parts he's been findin' lately."

We all cringed at the reminder of things we'd come across out at Harvey's ranch over the last few months. "Pieces and parts" summed it up in the least gruesome way possible.

Cornelius scooted forward on the bench seat. "I'd theorize that the solution for removing the steel rod from the detective's sphincter is several rounds of mistletoe therapy over the next twenty-four hours."

I agreed, pointing at Natalie. "Only *you* can save Christmas."

She glared back. "Why don't you try that experiment first and let me know how it turns out."

A loud snort came from the old man next to me. "Coop will shoot Sparky just for puckerin' up."

The back doors opened, the main subject of our teasing ushering us out one by one, while Reid helped Natalie and me down.

I told Reid to leave Santa's bag of presents in the snowcat for now, wanting to make sure the kids were in bed before sneaking their presents inside and stashing them under the tree.

Doc turned me toward the front door soon after my boots hit the snow. "Go check on the kids. I'll bring your duffel bag and Elvis."

I slipped and crunched up the front walk, smiling wide. We'd made it in time. For a moment up there on that snowy road, I'd almost lost hope.

Aunt Zoe hugged me when I joined her on the porch. "I'm glad you're here," she said and kissed my forehead.

"Even though I brought Reid?"

"Even though."

"Please try to be nice to him. Reid saved our bacon. Without him and his snowcat, we'd have had to turn around and slide back down Strawberry Hill with our fingers crossed on making it into Deadwood alive."

"I'll keep that in mind while I'm handling any sharp kitchen utensils in his vicinity."

I lowered my voice. "He has a 'special something' just for you."

Her gaze narrowed. "I've seen his 'special something' before. If he thinks I'm letting it within ten feet of me, he's got another *think* coming."

I laughed and hugged her again. "Does Dad know Reid's coming?"

"I just told him. Blake promised to keep his hands to himself and let me deal with this."

"Good."

"Your mother is in a panic, though."

"Why's that?"

"She doesn't think she has enough eggs for all of us."

"Eggs?" Only my mother would worry about eggs at a time like this. "Lucky for her I brought a chicken along."

"You brought Elvis?"

"I couldn't leave her at your place without Harvey there. Addy would've freaked out."

She nodded. "It would definitely be a blue Christmas without Elvis."

I grinned at her echo of my earlier thought. "Exactly."

"Head inside, baby girl. Hope just got your kids to bed. They're waiting for a kiss good night."

I started to open the door, but then hesitated as Reid crested the top porch step, curiosity making me slow to turtle speed.

"Merry Christmas, Zo," he said, his voice deeper than usual. I could hear the uncertainty in it. "Well, almost Christmas."

Aunt Zoe sniffed. "You're good, Martin. This was a very shrewd chess move on your part."

His arms spread wide. "I don't know what you're talking about."

"Don't even try to play innocent. If you thought you could come here and convince me to change my answer, you're wasting your time."

Her answer to what?

I opened my mouth to pry, but caught myself at the last moment. Slipping inside the house, I quietly closed the door behind me. I'd have to badger Aunt Zoe for details later when I had a chance to catch her alone.

The foyer smelled like fresh-baked apple pie. I drooled all over myself as I kicked off my boots. My mother came around the corner from the dining room as I was unbuttoning my coat. She looked radiant in the shiny gold dressing gown she wore only around the holidays. Her blond hair flowed over her shoulders, her cheeks warmed with a pink blush.

"I'm so glad to see you," she said, pulling me in for a squeeze. I could smell the rum on her. That explained the blush.

"I told you I'd make it," I said when she held me at arm's length.

"And I told you that blizzard was coming, but did you listen to me? Of course not. What do I know?"

"Let her be, Hope," my father said from behind her. A

Santa hat covered his black hair, the silver at his temples blending with the white furry trim. "She made it in before midnight. We're lucky to have her here at all with this storm."

I rushed into his arms, one of my favorite places, and snuggled against his soft red flannel shirt for a moment. Ah, there it was. Home sweet home.

"I brought Reid," I admitted right out of the gate.

"I heard."

I frowned up at him. "He saved the day, so please try to be good."

"Your aunt already gave me a lecture, and I agreed not to shoot him in the ass on sight."

Well, that was a start. "What about tomorrow?"

He kissed the top of my head before letting me go. "One day at a time, Goldilocks."

"I can't believe you brought five additional guests, Violet," Mom said, helping me take off my coat.

"I couldn't leave them alone on Christmas."

"Your heart always has been too big when it comes to lonely critters, human or not." She squeezed my chin. "We're going to need more eggs."

"You're in luck. I invited a chicken to Christmas, too."

Dad laughed and stepped around us, opening the front door in time to pull Natalie inside.

She gave both of my parents a kiss on the cheek. Doc followed shortly, shaking my father's hand and then letting my mother hug and coo about him while he charmed her with compliments.

I left the foyer, hurrying past the dining table and down the hallway, avoiding the living room in case Susan was lurking there. Addy and Layne shared my brother's old room whenever they came to stay at my parents, which was now equipped with bunk beds since Quint stayed at his condo the few days a year he was actually in town.

Addy squealed when I stepped through the doorway. She rolled out of bed and threw herself at me, wrapping me in her little arms when I lowered to her level. "I was so worried you wouldn't make it through the snow, Mom."

This moment had been worth the angst and frustrations of the last twelve hours. I held her tight and breathed her in, smelling the coconut-scented bubble bath that Mom kept in the spare bathroom for when my kids were visiting. I stroked my daughter's hair, soaking up her heated hug. While Addy and I shared the same hair color, unlike my thick curly mess, her hair always reminded me of blond corn silk.

"No blizzard is going to keep me from you two," I whispered. I swallowed the lump in my throat and smiled, holding out Buck the unicorn for her to take. "Guess who else I brought along?"

She took Buck and hugged him to her cheek. "Grammy already told us. You brought Natalie."

"I'm not talking about Nat. This special guest has a red comb, white feathers, and a poodle sweater."

"Elvis!" Addy jumped free of my arms, bouncing up and down around the room.

Dang. That silly chicken received as much joy at making it in time for Christmas as I had, maybe more.

I rose and looked at my son, who was sitting on the top bunk with his legs dangling over the side rail. "Hey, big guy, do I get a Christmas Eve hug or what?"

Layne tried to act cool and reserved with his damp dark blond hair combed back, but when I stepped closer and held up my arms, his face split in a big, puppy-loving grin. He bent forward and gave me a hug that lasted twice as long as usual.

"Don't do that again, Mom," he whispered in my ear before pulling away.

I wasn't sure what he meant, but I tweaked his chin

playfully. "I won't, sweetheart."

"Where's Doc?" he asked, frowning behind me toward the doorway.

"He's saying 'Hi' to your grandparents. Why?" I worried my lower lip. I thought my son had made it beyond being jealous of a man in my life when it came to Doc.

Layne's forehead creased. "Addy had a bad dream about him last night."

A shadow fell over my Christmas glow. Addy had been having dreams more and more lately that mirrored true events happening in my freak-filled world. Doc and I weren't sure if she was exhibiting signs of being able to see the future, the past, or both. There was also the distinct possibility that she was eavesdropping on our adult conversations and suffering from the side effects of a wild imagination. Of the two, I preferred the latter by far.

I looked at my daughter, who was twirling in the middle of the room, singing some song about taking a road trip with her chicken someday. She didn't seem to be bothered by her nightmare at the moment.

"Addy, what was your dream about?"

She stopped spinning and grabbed the bunk bed ladder to steady herself. Her head wobbling slightly, she told me in a breathless voice, "The monster's pets were attacking Doc and I couldn't save him."

I sat on that for a couple of breaths. "What monster?"

She scrunched up her face in thought. "It was hard to see it in the dark, but I remember it had orange eyes."

Orange eyes? A rush of panic flooded me. I clutched the railing next to Layne's legs. I knew a monster with orange eyes. He haunted me in the darkness, too.

"Addy, was the monster stinky?" I pressed. Did it have little horns on its head? Pustules covering its jet-black skin?

"I don't remember it stinking."

Lucky her. I could still smell the sulfur odor if I thought

too much about it.

"I mostly remember its pets," she continued. "At first I thought they were wolves, but then I realized they were bigger, more like ugly bears, with long teeth and claws."

Long teeth and claws? I'd also run into a couple of troublesome creatures that fit that description.

"Oh," she added, holding up her index finger. "They could also stand up on their three back legs. That made them really, really tall. They made Doc look like a kid."

"*Three* legs?" That was new.

"Yeah. One leg might have been a thick tail, though."

"How could you see these things so well in the dark?"

She shrugged. "Doc gave me his candle so I could find my way home."

A chill raced through me. I'd recently used a candle in my version of "the dark." Actually, I'd used Doc's candle in there, too. Was Addy tapping into my thoughts somehow?

"It was after he gave me his candle that the pets attacked Doc and started biting him."

"What bit me?" Doc asked, standing in the doorway with Elvis's crate in his hand. His expression sobered when he looked from Addy to me. His eyebrows rose.

I shook my head. I'd fill him in after the kids went to bed. Or maybe even after Christmas was over and life returned to its normal bizarre status quo.

Addy cried out and raced to Doc, hugging him around the waist. She beamed up at him. "I'm so glad you're here. I was afraid you'd miss Santa's visit."

Doc tugged playfully on a strand of hair next to her ear. "Not even a blizzard could keep your mom and me away tonight."

Addy detached herself, taking Elvis from Doc and freeing the chicken from the cage.

"Hey, Layne." Doc held out his fist toward Layne, who bumped it back with his own. "Have you been taking care of your sister?"

"Mostly. But she gets bossy. You know how girls are."

"Yeah, they're the worst," Doc joked, draping his arm around my neck. "Aren't you two kids supposed to be all snug in your beds by now and dreaming about dancing mice or something like that?"

"Dancing sugarplums," Addy corrected him.

"Right, dancing sugarplums." Doc winked at me. "One of my favorite sights."

"Well, well, well," said a sultry voice, dumping a bucket of ice water on our reunion. "Isn't this a cozy family scene?"

My shoulders tightened so fast that something cracked in my neck. I turned toward the door, my gunslinger glare cocked and loaded.

Susan leaned against the doorframe in a short red velvet robe with plenty of leg showing for this cold winter night. She set her sights above my head. "Finally, I get to meet the real Doc Nyce."

Chapter Eleven

Christmas … Just After Midnight

"Violet, quit pacing and come to bed." Doc patted the spot next to him on the queen-sized bed in my old bedroom.

I huffed once more, and then stepped out of the flannel pajama pants I'd thrown on earlier after we'd settled Cooper, Reid, Harvey, and Cornelius over at the Morgan house next door. Natalie had decided to sleep on the couch in my parents' living room. I had a feeling it was to put even more distance between her and a certain law dog, but she told me and my kids that she wanted to keep an eye out for Santa. Layne had given me a knowing look before scampering back to his top bunk bed. He'd recently informed me that he knew all about "Santa," but had promised not to ruin the fun for Addy.

After the kids had fallen asleep, Doc and I slipped the presents under the tree. Natalie, my parents, and Aunt Zoe watched, drinking hot buttered rum and sharing stories of Christmas past.

Thankfully, Susan hadn't come up from the basement to share a drink with everyone.

Since moving back home, she was staying in the same room I'd used while living off and on with my parents before relocating up to Deadwood with Aunt Zoe. My dad's man cave was down there, too, with a big-screen television and stereo to keep her entertained.

Susan also hadn't hit on Doc earlier in the kids' room.

She hadn't eaten him up with her eyes.

She hadn't slithered in close and tried to touch him.

She hadn't even flapped her long eyelashes at him.

All she'd done was smile and say, "It's nice to see you really do exist. I was beginning to wonder after all of Violet's silly games." Then she'd told me, "I need to talk to you in the morning, big sis," and left without another word.

Something was up. I could feel it in my gut, but I let it go. It was Christmas, and I wasn't going to cause a stir.

After finishing their drinks, my parents and Aunt Zoe had called it a night. Doc and I followed in their wake a short time later, leaving Natalie to settle in on the couch. Doc had wasted no time brushing his teeth and stretching out under the comforter on my bed.

I, on the other hand, couldn't sit still once we were alone. What was going on with my sister? I wasn't buying my mom's explanation that Susan was on her best behavior because of the holiday. Christmas had never derailed the destructive brat from her relentless mission to screw with my happiness before. No matter what my mom thought, a tiger couldn't change its stripes, a leopard couldn't shake its spots, and a snake was a snake, period.

I pulled off my sweater and tossed it on the end of the bed. "I'm telling you, Susan is up to no good." I slid in next to Doc beneath the flannel sheets. "Did she say anything to you when I went next door with Natalie to help get the guys settled in over there?"

"No. She didn't come upstairs at all as far as I know." He leaned on his elbow, watching me fluff and re-fluff my pillow, unable to poof it up just right. "Your sister probably took one look at me, saw how nuts I am about you, and figured that singing her siren song near me would be a waste of energy."

I smirked at him. "You're definitely nuts, but there has to be a reason for her not trying to seduce you."

"You do realize that you're exhibiting signs of paranoia,

right?"

I pulled the covers up to my chin. "My bet is she's biding her time before she delivers her next low blow."

"For example, an abnormal fear of being deceived is typical with paranoia sufferers."

I pulled my legs up, rubbing my cold heels on the warm sheets. "She's just waiting to catch me off guard, you'll see."

He glanced down at the hill I'd made under the covers. "The inability to relax is another telltale sign."

I flattened my legs and blew out a breath. "I'm not paranoid, Doc."

The small Christmas tree my mom had set up on my dresser shed a soft light on his smile. "Denial is a red flag. It goes hand-in-hand with the characteristic argumentative predisposition of a paranoid disorder."

"Yeah, well you'd be paranoid, too, if you'd endured the shit I have from Susan."

"Undoubtedly." His thumb traced my jawline, his gaze locking onto my mouth. "Merry Christmas, Boots. What's that little number you're wearing under the covers?"

Oh, yeah! Susan had me so distracted I'd forgotten about the gift with which I'd planned to surprise him once we were alone.

I peeled back the covers. "It's a little present for you."

"For me?" He whistled through his teeth, pushing the covers back further. He admired the skimpy Mrs. Claus lingerie getup first with his eyes and then with his fingers. "It's little, all right, and see-through in all of the right places. The velvet is a nice touch. All it's missing is bells and lights."

I snuggled closer to him. "I'd ask you to kiss me, but we don't have any mistletoe close by."

"Damn. I'll just have to kiss everywhere but your lips for now." He started with my neck and headed south, warming me up so much I didn't miss the covers. His beard stubble tickled my libido awake, spurring me to move against him for even more pleasure.

Outside the bedroom window, the wind whistled while snow pelted the glass. I wrapped my leg around him, my foot rubbing up and down his calf as his lips skimmed over my skin.

He groaned, lifting his face from the velvet and lace bra. "Woman, your foot is like a block of ice."

"I know. You need to heat me up."

I shifted and my knee collided with his thigh.

He grunted. "Hold still for a minute." He turned me onto my side and pulled me against him, spooning out his warmth up and down my back. His breath tickled my shoulder.

"There. That's better." His hand drifted south to my waist, his palm heating my goose bump–covered skin. "Why are you so cold?"

"My dad likes to keep the house chillier than Aunt Zoe does in the winter." I found his ankle with my frozen toes. "I usually wear flannel pajamas to bed when I sleep in here, but since you're in bed with me, I skipped the extra layers."

"I appreciate that." He nuzzled my neck, his hand sneaking inside the red velvet panties, rubbing over my hip. "Your bare skin is one of my favorite things."

I could tell. His body language left no doubts. I smiled and closed my eyes. "No pajamas means your job is to thaw my frozen parts."

His lips trailed along my shoulder. "I have just the thing to heat you up."

"Oh, really?"

"Uh-huh." He shifted away from me, making the bed move. The sound of paper crinkling made me open my eyes. What was he …

A small present appeared in front of my face. "Merry Christmas, Miss Frosty Toes."

I took the present from him and rolled onto my back, squeezing it through the wrapping paper. "It's squishy."

"I thought you said squeezing presents was off limits."

"It is when they're not my presents." I peeled off the paper. Holding up the thick bundle in the dim glow. "You got me socks?"

"Not just any socks, sweetheart. These are pure cashmere purple socks guaranteed to thaw those frozen nuggets currently wedged under my leg."

I giggled and reached down under the covers, pulling on one sock and then the other. "Wow, they're really warm." Turning so I faced him, I rubbed one sock-wrapped foot up and down his leg. "Is that better, you big baby?"

"Not quite." He hooked his hand behind my knee and pulled me tighter against him, his hips pressing deep into mine. "There, that's better."

"Why, Doc. I believe you're getting frisky with me. You do remember that we're in my parents' house, right?"

"Yep." He cupped my hip, sliding his fingers under the lacy hem of my velvet underwear again. His dark eyes sparkled along with the Christmas lights. "I have another present for you, Boots."

My body hummed to life as his fingers teased just out of reach. "Can I squeeze this one, too?"

"I don't know." He rocked against me. "Can you?"

I pushed him onto his back and moved on top of him. "We have to be quiet," I whispered. "My parents' room is across the hall."

"Did you lock the bedroom door?"

I lowered my mouth, hovering over his. "Nope."

One of his eyebrows climbed upward. "Don't you think we should?"

"Who's paranoid now?"

My lips brushed his, my tongue returning for seconds and thirds. He tasted like cinnamon and rum served with a splash of risky rebellion. Even though I was no virgin and my parents couldn't care less about my sex life, there was something about having Doc in the bedroom where I'd fantasized about boys for so many years that made me feel reckless.

He gripped my hips, rubbing against the red velvet. My kisses grew frenzied, mixed with smothered gasps and groans from both of us. I pulled the covers over our heads, plunging us into darkness. My mouth trailed down over his Adam's apple, along his collarbone, up to the shell of his ear. My hand drifted down over his stomach, pushing his briefs lower, squeezing and teasing until he started to arch off the bed.

"No," he complained when I drew my hand away.

I shimmied out of my underwear with lightning speed.

"Yes." I slid down his body, taking all he had to offer in one smooth move.

His breath caught, his body going completely still for several moments.

"What's wrong?" I asked, pulling down the covers. I listened to the house creak while the wind rattled the trees outside my window. "Did you hear something?"

He rolled me over onto my back, pressing me into the mattress with his body, never losing touch. "Yeah, I heard the angels sing there for a moment when you took me."

I giggled as he leaned down and grazed my neck with his mouth. "That sounds like some hokey pick-up line."

He moved slowly against me, keeping the bed from creaking while his teeth nipped at my collarbone. "I can't help it," he murmured in my ear. "You melted my brain with that hot little outfit. Wrap your legs around me, Vixen."

He was doing a hell of a job of melting me from the inside out, too. I did as told and pulled the covers back up over our heads, taking us back to our private world where I had Doc all to myself.

As the need inside of me ratcheted higher and higher, I clung to him and filled the dark with whispered adoration for his hard work and even harder body. When I arched and shuddered under his touch, he covered my mouth with his and soaked up my moan of pleasure. After a few more thrusts, his body stiffened. He collapsed on me, his muscles trembling from the aftershocks for a few more breaths.

"I can feel your heart pounding," I said, pulling down the covers again.

He turned onto his side, taking me with him. "That was the best Christmas present ever."

I smiled at him. "Well, Santa told me you were a good boy this year and deserved a little extra hubba-hubba with your presents."

His chuckle sounded low and sexy. "You certainly give the best hubba-hubba in town."

"You remember that if any of the other reindeer come around wanting you to help guide their sleigh tonight or any other night."

"Not going to happen." He traced my hairline. "I'm crazy in love with you, Boots."

Ah, hell. *Good-bye for good, heart. It was nice knowing you.*

Instead of telling him all of the sappy thoughts gushing from my smitten brain, I kissed him and took my time about it.

When I pulled away, he groaned and flopped onto his back, staring up at the ceiling. "Christ, woman. How do you do that with your lips alone?"

"I practiced long and hard."

He aimed a frown my way. "With whom?"

"The teddy bears up on the shelf in my closet. I'll be right back."

I slipped out of bed, grabbed my robe, and tiptoed down the hall to the bathroom. On the way back to my room, I checked on the kids. Both were sound asleep. I hoped they were dreaming of Santa and not some orange-eyed monster and its pets.

Back in my room, I pulled out a red satin camisole and matching panties that I'd stashed in my nightstand earlier. The hip-length top was still soft and sexy, but wouldn't shock the kids like my velvet and lace getup if they woke before me in the morning and stopped by my room.

Doc leaned on his elbow to watch while I shucked the velvet and lace brassiere and pulled the camisole over my head.

"Okay." I climbed back into bed in my satin pajamas, snuggling up to him. "Where were we?"

"I was warming you up." He brushed his fingers over the satin. "I like this, too."

"I thought you might." I caught his hand. "We need to get some sleep. Those two kids will be up at the butt crack of dawn wanting to open presents." Wrapping his arm around me, I settled back into our earlier spooning position.

"Mmmm, nice. So soft." He yawned, his hand cupping a handful of curves. "I can't wait to see the kids' faces when they see the presents Santa brought them." Doc had added to my Santa pile after the children had crashed, pulling several gifts from a bag he'd sent earlier with Aunt Zoe.

I stared at the small tree on my dresser until the lights blurred. "Doc?" I whispered, my eyes heavy.

"Hmmm?"

"I'm not paranoid. It's just that I love you and don't want to lose you." Not to Susan. Not to some bear-like monsters from Addy's dream world. Not to anyone or anything ever.

"You won't." He yawned again.

I wanted to believe him. I really did.

Chapter Twelve

Christmas … The Butt Crack of Dawn

Something was poking me in the shoulder.
I swatted at it, shifting away from it.
It poked me again, harder.

"Mom," a voice whispered in my ear.

"What?" It came out more of a groan than a word.

"Wake up! Santa came."

Doc shifted in the bed beside me, his hand sliding up my ribcage, settling under my breast. I started to scoot closer to him and then stopped cold.

Shit. We had an audience.

I opened my eyes.

Addy and Layne stood at my side of the bed, their gazes going back and forth between Doc and me.

My glance at Doc found his eyes still closed. His hand started to drift higher.

I let out a squeak and jackknifed upright. "Look at all of that snow," I said, pointing at the window.

While their attention was diverted, I nudged Doc awake. He blinked a couple of times and then his focus locked onto the kids as they turned back to us.

"Doc's in your bed again," Layne pointed out.

I couldn't read if he was unhappy about that or not by his poker face. "Uh, yeah, he sure is."

"Are your ribs still hurting?" Addy asked Doc, her forehead creased. "Mom said it would take awhile to heal."

His bruised ribs requiring a nighttime nurse was the reason we'd given for him being in my bed last week when the kids had found him by my side.

"They're a little sore yet." He shot me a questioning glance. "Did Santa come?"

Layne crossed his arms. "No boy has ever slept in this room with Mom before besides me."

When the kids were younger, I'd let them sleep in my room with me when we visited, but only one was allowed in bed next to me at a time. The other camped out on the floor in a sleeping bag. That's when I'd told Layne that he was the only boy who'd ever slept in the bed with me. I was surprised he remembered that detail after all of these years.

"Really?" Doc sat up. "Did you like this bed?"

"It was okay. Mom has cold feet though in the winter."

"Oh, boy, does she," Doc agreed with a chuckle, dodging my pinching fingers. "Did your mom kick you when you slept with her? Because I think she bruised my shin last night."

"She moves her legs a lot like she's running from something," Addy explained. "One time she kneed me in the back so hard it made me scream awake."

"It wasn't that hard," I defended. "And it was more of a squeak than a scream." I'd been stressed out at the time about my old job at the dealership and a customer who was giving me hell about a car repair gone bad. Those problems paled in comparison to the shitstorms I faced these days.

"Hey!" Natalie said from the doorway. She had her hair pulled back in a ponytail and my mom's thick terrycloth wildflower robe belted around her waist. "Are we opening Santa's presents or what?"

Both kids grinned wide at her before turning to me again. "Can we, Mom?"

"Of course! Go with Nat and start dividing up the presents. Doc and I will be right out."

The kids took off in a flash.

Nat made room for them to pass, watching them go.

"You owe me one for that distraction, babe."

"Agreed," I said and shooed her away. "Close the door behind you, please." I didn't need to have my parents stopping by for a visit while we were still in bed.

After the door was shut, I hopped out of bed and pulled my yoga pants on over my satin skivvies.

Doc sat up in bed, watching me. "Oh man. Now I'm going to be thinking about that slippery satin all day long."

I grinned, grabbing my thick sweater. "Are you going to get dressed or what?"

"So, I'm the only man who's ever slept with you in your bed, huh?" His smile had a cocky glint to it.

I pulled the sweater over my head. "Yeah. You want to make a big deal out of it?"

"I might. A trophy would be nice. Maybe a crown with a sexy little ceremony later to commemorate it. Your red satin panties optional, of course."

I laughed, pulling the covers off of him. "Come on. The kids are waiting. We have presents to open."

Even though I was mostly dressed when Doc crawled out of bed, he still managed to beat me out the door, catching my hand and dragging me along behind him.

Natalie, my parents, and Aunt Zoe were waiting for us in the living room with the kids. Susan was missing, much to my relief. Harvey came knocking as we were settling down, joining in the Santa fun. According to him, Reid and Cornelius were starting to rattle around next door when he'd left, and Cooper was in the shower.

A glance in Natalie's direction at that last bit about Cooper ran smack-dab into a steely glare. I shrugged with a grin and focused on my kids and their presents.

The Tasmanian devil had nothing on Addy and Layne when it came to tearing through presents. Squeals of delight filled my ears for the next thirty minutes or so, including one from my mom when she saw the new robe covered in stars and moons that Aunt Zoe had given her.

The expensive bottle of imported mead from Poland that I special ordered for one of Doc's gifts earned me a heart-palpitating smolder. He leaned over and kissed my cheek, whispering, "You do remember that mead is the elixir of love, right?"

I licked my lips in reply, eager to try the mix of fermented honey and raspberry along with him.

After the chaos had died down, I escaped to the kitchen in search of caffeine, leaving Doc on the floor with Addy. He was helping her assemble a portable veterinarian toy my mom had added to the "from Santa" gifts that included tiny dogs and cats for Addy to examine. Meanwhile, Layne and Natalie sat together on the couch looking through a book about legendary monsters that Doc had given him under the Santa guise.

Aunt Zoe and my dad were already in the kitchen when I arrived, whispering heatedly by the sink. My father's crossed arms and set jaw left little doubt about the topic of their discussion.

"You two better be nice to Reid when he gets here," I said, grabbing two mugs from the cupboard. "He saved my bacon last night."

"That's not what we're arguing about," Aunt Zoe said with a sniff. "At least not in the way you think."

"What's going on, then?"

"Blake wants to go with Reid to the store in my place and I don't believe it's a good idea."

I set the mugs on the counter in front of the coffee pot that was in the midst of brewing. The scent of fresh coffee woke up my inner smartass. I grinned at her. "You think Dad will ditch the body in a snow bank on the way back?"

Dad shot me a conspiratorial wink. "Who says I'll let him live long enough to even make it to the store?"

"Blake," Aunt Zoe said. "I know you're being a

protective big brother right now, and I really appreciate it, but you need to let this go. I have Reid under control."

"Really?" Dad said, grabbing his sister's hand and holding out her arm. "Then explain this."

I joined them, taking a closer look at the charm bracelet wrapped around her wrist. The bracelet was made of woven silver heart links. I whistled in appreciation at the charms decorating the heart bracelet, each adorned with different-colored jewels.

"Did Reid give you this?" I asked. Was it the "special something" he'd mentioned last night?

"Yes. He had me open it on the porch before we came inside."

It was breathtaking. No wonder he'd wanted to give it to her in person.

"What do these represent?" I asked, pointing at the unique charms.

"Each symbolizes different strong women in mythology or history." She pointed at a skull charm with a tiny ruby in its mouth. "This gold one is Itzpapalotl, the Aztec skeletal warrior goddess. And this one with the shield and amethyst center represents Athena, the Greek goddess of wisdom and war."

"I love it." Reid knew my aunt well. "What about the rest?"

She turned her wrist so I could see each one. "Joan of Arc with a piece of aragonite at the base of her sword. Freyja, a goddess from Norse mythology who's associated with love, sex, beauty, fertility, war, and death is here with a sapphire. Here is Bellona, the Roman goddess of war with a ruby in her shield. This one with the jade piece represents the Maya moon goddess. And this last one with the jasper stands for one of my favorite women from history. It's Khutulun, the thirteenth-century Mongol princess. Marco Polo wrote about her in his chronicles. She was a skilled warrior who vowed to marry only the man who could defeat her in wrestling."

"Did any guy ever beat her?"

"No, but she's said to have won thousands of horses from would-be suitors. She did eventually marry a warrior. Some have said that true love was her downfall, while others claimed she was forced into a liaison for strategic reasons."

I stepped back, impressed as hell. "Reid handpicked these charms for you?"

She scowled, nodding. "He said he had it custom made for me."

"Damn," I said, chuckling. "That man is smooth."

"Yeah," Dad said with a huff. "Slick as they come. He always has been when it comes to schmoozing your aunt."

Aunt Zoe wrinkled her nose at my dad.

Mom breezed into the kitchen, her purse in hand. "Reid is here. He's game to drive me to the store. Are you ready?" she asked Aunt Zoe.

"Zoe isn't going," Dad said. "I am."

"Oh, dear," my mom replied, her forehead lining.

When Aunt Zoe started to object, Dad held up his hand. "I promise to be on my best behavior."

"Blake, I don't want—"

"It's high time Reid and I talked this out and got a few

things straight, man to man."

"I still don't think—"

"Don't worry. We'll take Violet with us."

I did a double take. "We will?"

My father nodded. "You can make sure I keep my hands to myself and not throttle the bastard for breaking my sister's heart."

"I will?" I repeated, not sure this was such a good idea. I hadn't even had a cup of coffee yet. Taking me out in public was a potential life-threatening hazard. Rabid dogs were nicer to strangers than me sans caffeine.

Mom looked at me and then down at my sweater and yoga pants before focusing on my hair. "Well, hurry up, Violet. I want to make a couple of quiches for breakfast and I need more eggs."

I smirked. Her lack of eggs must have haunted her in her sleep. "I really think Aunt Zoe should go in my place."

"Nope," Dad said. He turned me around by the shoulders and nudged me toward the living room. "Get cracking. The bus leaves in five minutes."

"It's a snowcat," I corrected.

"Go!"

I did as told, changing in lightning speed. I was sitting on the bed pulling on my snow boots when Doc came into the bedroom.

"I hear you've been recruited to play referee this morning."

I blew out a breath. "Gah! Like I want to be in the middle of my dad and Reid having it out about Aunt Zoe."

"Before you go, I have something for you."

"Is it a portable shark cage? I could use a good-sized tranquilizer gun." I stood as Doc pulled a mid-sized box wrapped in silver paper with a red bow from under the bed.

"How many presents do you have stashed under there?"

He handed me the gift. "Merry Christmas."

It felt weighty. I shook it and smiled. "Is it a bunch more socks?"

He laughed. "Open it."

I tore off the paper with zeal, time being short and all, and opened the box lid. I gasped. An indigo cashmere trench coat filled the box. I lifted it out and laid it on the bed, running my fingers over the soft, luxurious fabric. "It's beautiful."

"Try it on," he urged, his hands jammed in his jeans' front pockets.

"Doc, this is too much." It couldn't have been cheap, not with the name brand on the inside tag.

"You needed another coat. Our adventures back in Slagton obliterated your red one."

I slipped it on, adjusting the classic collar, smoothing my hand down the double-breasted front. It fit like it was made for me. "It's perfect."

His eyes narrowed. "Do you really like it? You're not just saying that, right? Because I can return it for another style or color."

I nearly tackled him in a rushed hug. "I love it." I kissed him hard and then stepped back and did a little twirl, mimicking my daughter from the previous night. "It will look amazing with my purple cowboy boots."

His eyes sparkled. "I know. I have a few new fantasies starring you, your boots, and that coat."

I returned to him and wrapped my arms around his neck, pressing him back against the wall. "Kiss me, *mon amour.*"

"*Cara mia*, that's French." He looked down at my coat. "I can't get to your arm to kiss it."

"Will my lips do?" I puckered up.

"*Ay yi yi*, these lips." He cupped my face and gave me a scorching kiss that burned clear to my cold toes.

"Violet!" My dad's voice boomed down the hall. "Let's

go. Your mom is waiting."

I sighed and pulled away. "Can I wear it to the store?"

"It's your coat, Tish."

After one more quick kiss and a breathy, "Thank you, Gomez," I raced out of the bedroom. My worries about playing referee between my dad and Reid had eased for the moment.

Mom raised her eyebrows as I joined her in the foyer. "New coat?"

"Doc got it for me."

She smiled wide. "He's a keeper."

I agreed. I was seriously considering locking Doc in the basement and never letting him out around the rest of the female population again. "It will look great with the new Ferragamo pumps you bought me, too," I said, kissing her cheek. My shoe supplier had fed my addiction with another hit, this time a pale pink, low-heeled pump.

Susan sauntered into the foyer as Mom reached for the door. My happy balloon deflated a bit at the sight of her form-fitting silver sweater dress. She looked like a sexy strand of tinsel bordered with blood red lips on top and spiky boots on the bottom.

I tried not to roll my eyes, but couldn't help myself. "Jeez, Susan. This isn't the Playboy Bunny holiday party."

"Jealous much?" she taunted, standing up straighter so that her perky boobs practically poked out my eyes.

Mom sighed. "You two knock it off. We have guests."

The silver strumpet looked toward the living room, her grin edging on feral. "We haven't had this much testosterone here for Christmas since that all-boy choir stopped by to sing carols when Violet and I were in high school."

I grimaced. "Those were little boys."

"And these are all big handsome men." She purred.

I narrowed my eyes. "Keep your hands to yourself."

"Mind your own business," she snapped back.

"Girls!" Dad said, breaking things up before we degenerated to our usual claws and hair-pulling routine.

"Sweetie," Mom said to Susan. "We'll be back soon. Would you be a dear and help your Aunt Zoe cut up some fruit for breakfast while I'm gone?"

"Yes, Mother." She looked back at me. "That's a pretty fancy coat, big sis. We need to talk."

"Talking never goes well for us. I think avoidance is a better plan for today." Without giving her a chance to nip at me in return, I followed my parents out the door to where Reid and his snowcat sat idling.

My father's shoulders tightened at the sight of Aunt Zoe's ex. He laced his fingers and cracked his knuckles.

"Dad," I warned. "You promised Aunt Zoe."

"I'll be good. But first, I'm going to explain a thing or two to Mr. Fireman about starting fires he can't put out."

My father had plenty of muscle to back up that statement, but Reid spent his working hours pumping iron and lugging big hoses around. The last place I wanted to be this morning was ringside while two hard-headed men traded blows.

"That's just splendid," I mumbled as I headed toward the snowcat's back doors. "Merry freaking Christmas, everyone."

Chapter Thirteen

Susan is up to something," I told my mom as we settled on opposite bench seats in the back of the snowcat. "I can feel it in my gut."

She sighed with all the drama of a soap opera star and zipped her white winter coat up to her striped scarf. "Violet Lynn, why do you insist on starting fights with your sister? Just once, could we have a nice holiday without all of the yelling?"

Reid and Dad climbed inside, fastening their seat belts. The silence up front weighed heavy. I could practically feel the tension in the cab.

I leaned forward, lowering my voice. "I'd love to have a happy family Christmas, Mother, but why does Susan want to talk to me?"

"Maybe she wants your big-sister advice on a job or a man, have you thought of that?"

I cackled a little too loudly. Reid shot me a worried frown in the rearview mirror. "That would be advice on how to steal *my* man and make me lose my latest job."

"Violet," Dad reprimanded without turning in his seat. This Susan song-and-dance between my mom and me was an old routine of ours, dating back decades. He'd witnessed it too many times to count.

I blew out a breath. "Sorry, Mom. Surely, though, you must understand my being apprehensive when it comes to Susan's motives."

She nodded. "However, I don't think this constant negativity is good for your psyche. You need to find a way to expel your toxic emotions in a more constructive way."

"Constructive how?" I could crochet a noose. Better yet, macramé was the way to go. Knotted twine would hold Susan's weight without breaking.

"Yoga is great for relaxation." Mom rested her elbows on her knees. She shot a glance toward the front, leaning closer to me. "It's excellent for your sex life, too."

I flinched like I'd been stung. "Oh, Mom. Did you have to go there?"

"These are things you need to learn as you age. I can move in ways now that I couldn't ten years ago. Believe me, your father really appreciates my flexibility. And as a bonus, several positions are good for more than just stretching, if you know what I mean." She wiggled her eyebrows at me.

"For the love of everything holy, don't do that eyebrow thing when you're talking about carnal relations with my father."

"I can't help it. He's a stud."

"That's enough. We're done here." I sat back and made an X with my fingers, warding her off.

She shrugged, sitting back. "Just remember that tip. Doc will appreciate it." Without missing a beat, she smiled toward the front. "Reid, I can't thank you enough for taking me to the store. It's very kind of you to help out like this."

Reid half-turned and hit her with one of his charming, heart-steaming smiles. "My pleasure. It's the least I could do for allowing me to join your family for the holiday."

Dad cleared his throat. "Reel in your hose, hotshot. That spitfire is mine."

Grinning, Reid faced forward again, focusing on the road. "Where to, Blake?"

"Take a right at the stop sign."

We cruised along making small talk for a few minutes about the heavy flakes that were still falling, how much snow the hills were hit with overnight, and how fortunate we were to have a store so close that was open on

Christmas morning.

We'd almost made it to the store when my dad frowned at Reid. "Zoe needs a reliable man. Someone who is interested in more than just her bed."

Of all the flying reindeer! Couldn't Dad have waited until Mom and I were in the store? I started to open my mouth and request a stay of execution, but Mom kicked me in the shin. When I gave her a what-the-hell look while rubbing my shin, she mimed zipping her lips.

"But I just want to—"

She kicked me again.

I wrinkled my upper lip at her and scooted toward the back of the snowcat, out of reach of her hard-toed boots.

"I asked her to marry me," Reid announced.

Dad and I both did a double-take.

"You did?" I blurted out.

"When?" Dad asked.

"A couple of weeks ago." He looked in the rearview mirror at me. "After the Deadwood Chamber of Commerce holiday party."

"Ah ha!" I pointed at him. "That was the night she lost her hair comb in your pickup, wasn't it?"

He focused back out the windshield. "Uh, yeah. We were … umm … clearing the air on a few things in the privacy of my pickup."

More like steaming up the air, I'd bet. Aunt Zoe had thick hair. Those combs didn't fall out without some help.

"That's when I popped the question," Reid continued.

"What did she say?" Mom asked.

"Nothing at first. Then she sucker-punched me in the breadbasket and told me to take her home."

I cringed on his behalf. Dang, Aunt Zoe hadn't said a word to me about his proposal.

Dad chuckled. "That's my sister for you."

"Isn't that the night Doc took you to the hospital for a

hand x-ray after you'd clocked Dominick Masterson?"

Reid nodded. "It wasn't one of my finer hours."

"Masterson is that friendly guy who showed up at the family dinner?" Dad asked, turning to me for the answer.

"Too friendly when it comes to Zo," Reid said.

"He's trouble," I told my dad.

"He seemed nice enough."

"You looked at him through the back door window, Dad. You have no idea what he's capable of when it comes to Aunt Zoe. Trust me, he's bad juju for our family."

Dad's eyes narrowed, questioning. Something in my expression must have given him the answer he was looking for, because he nodded and looked back to Reid.

"So, Zoe rejected you and yet you still came down here to see her?"

"I wanted to give her something."

"Are you referring to the bracelet she's wearing this morning or something else?" Dad pressed.

Poor Reid. My father wasn't going to remove his teeth from Reid's hide without dragging him through the dirt a bit first.

"Mainly the bracelet." He smiled at Dad. "She's wearing the bracelet today, huh?"

"Yeah. You could have sent it to her in the mail."

Reid shook his head. "It wasn't the gift so much as the need to see her face when she opened it."

"What exactly were you looking for?" Dad asked.

"I wanted to see if I had a chance at striking oil, or if I was just digging a deeper grave."

I scooted closer to the front again. "Which is it? Could you tell?"

"Well, Zo has one hell of a poker face, so it's hard to know for sure."

"Damn." I'd long ago put my money on Reid. He'd won me over back in August when he'd picked on Cooper while my beloved old Bronco burned into a smoking mess.

Reid winked at me in the mirror. "But her thank-you last night had plenty of spark."

I cheered.

Dad shot me a small scowl.

"Come on, Dad. Reid wants to marry her. Surely that's enough to convince you that he's not going to love 'er and leave 'er again."

"Officially, I didn't leave Zo," Reid defended. "She kicked me out."

A grunt came from my dad. "Because you were a chicken shit when it came to commitment."

"You're right, but I had just come off a vicious divorce and I'd run out of faith in the notion of marriage."

"And now you've changed your mind?" Mom asked.

"When it comes to Zo, yes." His expression looked bleak in the rearview mirror. "Listen, Blake. I know what a dipshit I was before. I know I'll be lucky to win your sister back. But if I do, trust me, I'm not going to blow it again."

"Good." Dad pointed out the windshield. "Take a left into that parking lot. The store is around the side."

"How can I help you win Aunt Zoe back?" I asked, eager to play cupid.

"By keeping your nose out of your aunt's business," Dad said, beating Reid to the punch. His grin took the sting out of his reply.

Mom patted my knee. "I've found that things work themselves out if you give them enough time and space."

"Oh, really?" I guffawed as we pulled into the minimart's parking lot. "And how's that working for you when it comes to Susan and me thirty-two years later?"

Her gaze hardened. "Violet Lynn, you are impossible some days. You have so many new wonderful things happening in your life right now, but you just can't see the sunshine through the gnarled old trees."

Reid and Dad opened their doors, stepping out.

"That's because I've been stabbed in the back too many times to count."

"You need to let all of that negative energy from your past go," she advised as the back doors opened. "Focus on where you have it good in life, like with Doc and your family, before you go and screw it up again."

"Again?" I growled at the roof. "Susan is the one who screwed up my chance at a family in the past, not me."

"Would you please stop playing the victim for a minute and try to look at it from an outsider's perspective?"

"Okay. How's this? Violet Parker's slutty sister seduced the father of Violet's unborn children and decided the most appropriate place to fornicate with him was in Violet's bed. What do you think? Newspaper worthy?"

"Not even close. Nobody uses the word 'fornicate' any more. It's old fashioned. You need to get with the times."

I cursed under my breath while I followed her down from the snowcat.

"Let it go, Goldilocks," Dad said to me as he steadied me on the packed snow. "Today is not the day to fight this battle with her."

"I've let this go too long. You stay out here with Reid." I stormed after my mom, yelling over my shoulder, "And be nice to him!"

The aroma of freshly made coffee greeted me inside the store. My need for caffeine had me gnashing my teeth as I looked for Mom. Overhead, a tinny version of "Jingle Bells" played through the speakers, strumming my nerves.

The minimart was mostly empty except for a few stragglers, including a grizzled-looking, older guy wearing camouflage from neck to toe except for his Santa Claus hat. He was standing several cooler doors down from my mom, scanning the single soldiers of beer through the glass. In one hand he held a jar of salsa, in the other a jumbo bag of tortilla chips.

"Mom." I joined her in front of the cooler doors. "Please explain to me how an outsider's perspective makes a difference on Susan boinking Rex behind my back."

Camo-Claus glanced our way, his focus lingering on my mother's butt. Her yoga was paying off yet again.

"It's simple, really. Because of your sister's interference, you have learned how to discern a good man from a loser."

Talk about making a leap! "So, in your eyes, Susan did a good thing?"

She made a face. "I wouldn't use the word 'good' in this case. 'Beneficial' seems more fitting."

What was with her and this new fun-with-words game? More to the point, "Why do you always take Susan's side?"

Mom sighed. "There are no sides, dear."

"Bull hockey." I crossed my arms. "Every time Susan does something to screw me over, you turn it around and make it part my fault."

"Language, Violet." She smiled apologetically at Camo-Claus.

"I didn't use any bad words!"

"And lower your voice." She grabbed two cartons of eggs from the cooler. "We're in a store, you know." She handed me the eggs and then reached in the cooler again.

"Fine," I said several decibels lower, clutching the egg cartons. "But I want an answer. Why do you always place half the blame on me when Susan is clearly the one who is at fault?"

She placed two more cartons of eggs on top of the others, forcing me to stack them up to my chin so I didn't drop any. "I believe there are two sides to every story, and it's best to hear both before passing judgment, especially when it comes to my children."

"And what was Susan's side of the story for sleeping with Rex? That she was protecting me?"

Susan had given me that bullshit excuse before, explaining that she'd been showing me via a visual demonstration of how inadequate Rex was as a father figure.

I glanced over my mom's shoulder. The old guy with the chips and salsa stared at us openly now. He should pull up a chair and bust open that bag.

"She said that she fell in love with him," Mom explained.

I gaped. "And that was enough for you to forgive her?"

"It's not my place to forgive her. It's yours, if you want to move on with your life."

"Yeah, that's not going to happen."

"Violet, forgiveness will set you free of this negativity that keeps your aura blotchy with shadows."

"Chinese checkers! Have you been hanging out with Cornelius and bumming his aura pills?"

"There are no such things." She turned back to the cooler, holding her chin. "Do you think I should get more eggnog?"

"It's on sale," Camo-Claus told her.

She graced him with another smile, making him blush. "And what a bargain, too."

I grunted at their little flirting display. "So, Susan believes she fell in love with Rex all of those years ago. How did she explain sleeping with my other boyfriend, then? The one after Rex? Wait, let me guess, she twisted her ankle in those thigh-high hooker boots she liked to wear and accidentally fell onto his Yule log?"

Mom gasped. "Really, dear. Do you think this gentleman wants to hear such things on Christmas morning?"

"I don't mind," he said with a grin.

My mother tittered. "You'll have to excuse my daughter. She's trying to work through some negative issues in her life."

He looked at me, sizing me up. "Pessimism will turn you into a bitter old prune long before your time. You should try smiling when you talk. It's hard to be upset when you smile."

"Thank you, Mr. Camo-Claus," I said through a toothy grin.

He winced. "Well, you're a might bit purtier when your eyes aren't bugging out so much, anyway." He focused back on my mom. "Outside of that creepy clown look she's sporting, I can see where she gets her good looks."

"Oh, you." Mom waved him away. She grabbed a carton of eggnog and tucked it inside the front of my coat. "All I'm saying is that when it comes to your sister and Rex, I understand how people will move heaven and earth for love. You should comprehend that concept now that you have Doc."

Yeah, yeah, yeah. Maybe I'd gone so far as to put my lifelong friendship with Natalie on the line for Doc, but Natalie wasn't sleeping with him when I'd had sex with Doc the first time. She'd only staked a claim on him.

A claim that I blatantly ignored, though.

I shook off the guilt gorilla that had made itself at home on my chest for a moment there. "So, she fell in love with the creep. Dammit, I was pregnant with Rex's kids at the time. Couldn't she have told me how she felt instead of screwing him first? And why *my bed*? What was wrong with the back seat of his car or some skanky hotel room?"

Camo-Claus ripped open his bag of chips. "Hell, any flat surface will do in a pinch," he said and stuffed a handful of corn chips in his mouth.

Mom pointed her thumb at him, her mouth pinched. "Way to go, Violet. Now you're going to have the neighbors talking about us."

"You don't even know who he is! Criminy, you'd

probably take his side over mine if we got into a brawl."

Camo-Claus held up his bag of chips, grinning through beard crumbs. "I'm more of a make-love-not-war type of guy."

Mom grabbed me by the shoulder of my coat and dragged me over to the milk cooler. "Violet Lynn, I'd hoped you'd have this figured out now that your kids are a little older, but I can see that you're too stubborn to understand the truth about your sister."

"That she's a man-stealing, toy-burning brat?"

"Besides that."

"Ha! So you admit that she's a weasel."

"I admit that my youngest child has some problems she's dealing with, yes."

"The problem being she's psycho."

"Name calling doesn't fix anything." She grabbed two gallons of milk from the cooler, kicking the door shut with her foot. "Now you listen, child, and you listen good, because I'm not going to say this again."

"I'm all ears and eggs."

"I can't give up on your sister. She's my child, just as you are. We all do things in life that throw kinks into our plans. Like you, I got pregnant with Susan by accident. Also like you, I have done what I could to make the most of my life since then, raising my children to the best of my abilities. I'm not a perfect mother and I know it, trust me. I also understand that you want me to stand here and agree with you that Susan is broken. However, I have to keep trying with her, because I love Susan just as I love you and Quint."

"But what about—"

"I'm not finished." She led the way to the counter. "If I start openly choosing sides, I'll lose Susan completely. I'm not blind when it comes to her crimes against you. My job is to try to help her become a better person through love and support." We got in line behind Mr. Camo-Claus, who was paying for his Feliz Navidad supplies. "That doesn't mean I love you any more or less."

I sighed, shifting so the corner of the eggnog carton wasn't jabbing into my boob. "Sometimes it just feels like you pick on me more than her."

"Do you understand how strong you are?"

"Are you referring to my muscles or my body odor?"

"Neither, wiseacre. Since you first started walking, you showed signs of a fierce independence. I believe that inner force is why you have struggled so much with finding a suitable partner."

"Let's not rehash my rotten history with men today." We'd be standing here for hours if she started down that road.

"You're a strong woman, Violet Lynn. Not just any man will do. Rex was certainly not the caliber of man you needed. Your father and I could see that from the get-go, but you had to find that out for yourself. In some ways, it was a relief when Susan drove you two apart."

I started to object, but she held up her gallon of milk to stop me.

"If she hadn't, I feared you might've stayed with the jerk through thick and thin because you were pregnant with his kids. Thanks to your sister's seduction, you have two lovely children and yet are free of a loser who would've only dragged you down."

I sniffed. "He is a major piece of shit."

"Sounds like you're lucky to be rid of him," Camo-Claus added over his shoulder as he collected his change.

"*And* you have Doc now," Mom added. "Don't you think it's time to move on and let go of your past woes?"

"I'd love to, but Rex has other ideas lately. Do you know anyone I can hire to perform a contract kill?"

Camo-Claus pulled a business card from his vest pocket

and handed it to me. "Merry Christmas, ladies," he said and tipped an imaginary cowboy hat before heading out into the snow.

I looked at his card and chuckled.

Mom leaned closer, trying to read the card. "He's not really a killer, is he?"

Takes one to know one, I thought, and stuffed his card in my coat pocket. "He's a taxidermist."

For a moment, I entertained the notion of having Rex stuffed. I could use him to practice my batting skills.

Mom put the two jugs of milk on the counter, and then helped me offload the eggs and eggnog.

While the clerk rung us up, she beamed at me. "Did you see Doc's face this morning while he watched Addy and Layne open presents?"

"No." I'd been busy watching my kids, too. "Why?"

"He loves your kids. Trust me, Doc will be ten times the father Rex could've ever hoped to be."

"Don't be counting chickens before they're hatched, Mom. We're not married yet."

She handed the clerk a wad of cash. "I know, but I have a feeling wedding bells will be in your future very soon."

I grabbed the bag with the eggs and one of the milk jugs. "Keep that to yourself, please. I don't want you and Dad scaring Doc away with a bunch of talk about commitment and raising my kids."

She grabbed the other gallon of milk and the eggnog. "I'm more worried about *you* running off than him."

"I thought we agreed you weren't going to start in on me about my lousy history with the male sex." I shouldered open the door, holding it for her.

"Not today, dear. It's Christmas."

"Thank Santa for that."

She paused on the way past me. "But have you considered that Doc might want a child of his own someday with the woman he loves?"

I shuddered at the notion. Raising twins on my own had burned me out on the idea of babies. They were cute to hold, but I liked giving them back these days.

While reliving the soul-sucking middle of the night feedings and the frustration of day-after-day teething whines, I followed my mom to the snowcat, where Reid was showing my dad something behind the blade.

If Doc wanted another kid, that could be a major snag in this happily-ever-after fantasy of mine. I'd closed the doors to my baby-making factory after Addy and Layne popped out, and I didn't plan on reopening the plant ever again.

Chapter Fourteen

I spent the next few hours ducking Susan so many times that I felt like quacking.

After eating some of my mom's blue ribbon–winning bacon and cheddar cheese quiche, and then letting the kids open a few more presents that weren't from the North Pole, I joined Aunt Zoe, Harvey, and my mom in the kitchen. Christmas dinner preparations were the main topics of discussion initially as the three of them got a rhythm going, and while my cooking skills were shitty at best, my dishwashing abilities were legendary. Not to mention that staying within range of the oven kept me away from Susan, who also made a habit of avoiding anything having to do with the culinary arts.

One way or another, I was determined to get through the day without ruining Christmas, and that meant keeping my distance from my sister. My mother might have made a strong case at the minimart for pardoning Susan's enthusiasm for bareback riding my boyfriends, but I wasn't naïve enough to forget the tinsel tart's ability to wreak havoc in my life in general.

"You tryin' to rinse all the color off that plate, Sparky?" Harvey asked, dishtowel in hand.

"Shush up and dry." I shoved the dripping plate at him.

He took the plate and grinned in the direction of my mom, who was rolling out a piecrust over on the bar. "Did she get her quick temper from you or her pa?"

Mom pushed a loose strand of blond hair away from her face, smearing flour on her cheek in the process. "Blake always says Violet is a chip off Zoe's block."

Aunt Zoe looked up from the prime rib she was checking for temperature. "She does have the stubborn streak that runs deep in our family line."

And a killing streak, too, I thought as I scrubbed out the pot in which Harvey had boiled potatoes.

"Make sure ya save those meat drippins," Harvey told her. "I'll need 'em for my Yorkshire pudding and the gravy for the taters."

I licked my lips, remembering the last time he'd made Yorkshire pudding. Forty-plus years of playing bachelor had turned Harvey into one hell of a cook. If it weren't for Doc, I'd pester the ol' boy to move in with me and the kids to take care of our bellies.

"Speaking of family business," I said while rinsing out the pot, "a little birdy told Mom and me today that you recently turned down a marriage proposal."

Aunt Zoe froze.

Harvey hooted. "Well, slap the dog and spit in the fire."

"Is that true?" I asked, handing the pot to Harvey.

She shoved the prime rib back in the oven and slammed the door. "I'm going to clock Martin in his glass jaw for running his big fat yap." Scowling, she pointed the thermometer at me. "You need to keep your lips zipped about that. Nobody else needs to know about it, not even Doc."

"Blake knows," Mom said as she cut out a pattern in the pie dough.

"Why didn't you tell me?" I dried my hands with a corner of Harvey's towel.

"Well, for one, I turned him down, so it's a moot point. For another, I didn't figure it was anyone else's business. Apparently, Reid thinks otherwise."

"He did find a way to join us for Christmas," Mom observed, fitting the dough on top of the heap of cherries in the pie pan. "Something tells me he didn't hear your rejection in his heart."

Aunt Zoe scoffed. "He should've. I did my damnedest to punch it in there."

"Don't be mad at Reid." I dropped onto one of the bar stools across from my mom, who was pinching the edge of the crust. "He was only explaining to Dad what his intentions are this time around."

Mom giggled. "Reid did share your response to his proposal, which couldn't have been easy in front of the three of us."

Poor Reid. I'd been witness to more than one dose of humiliation doled out by my aunt. The first time was when she'd punched him hard enough to knock him off a cliff. The second happened after we hauled him back up from the ledge below the cliff. He'd asked her to consider becoming a couple again and she'd turned him down, hopped in her pickup, and driven away, leaving me behind to keep Reid company. Then there was today's admission. Coming clean in front of my parents had to have been up there with waltzing down Deadwood's Main Street in nothing but his favorite red underwear. It was a wonder Reid even wanted me around anymore.

Aunt Zoe sprinkled bacon bits on the mushroom caps stuffed with cream cheese. "What did he tell you?"

"That you sucker-punched him," Mom told her, brushing the crust with an egg white.

I added, "And that you demanded to be taken home immediately. I still can't believe you didn't tell me. I tell you everything."

"That's a bunch of hogwash," she said.

"Which part?" Harvey asked.

"Both Reid's proposal and Violet saying she tells me everything. She kept Doc a secret from me for weeks." Setting the pan of mushroom caps aside, Aunt Zoe waved me over. "Finish up these deviled eggs, will you?"

"Violet's the queen of secrets. She always has been." Mom sprinkled sugar on top of the pie and then wiped her hands on her apron. "There. Do you think we have enough pies?"

I grew up needing to keep secrets. Having Susan always searching for my emotional gold to plunder and destroy made being secretive a must. "Mom, you already had four pies made when we arrived last night. I told you we don't need any more."

"I disagree, Sparky." Harvey winked at Mom. "Ya can never have enough cherry pie. Ain't that right, Hope?"

"That's right, Willis."

"Plus," I continued, "there are the Christmas cookies the kids made. Oh, and that powdered sugar and chocolate cereal stuff that makes a big mess of my kids' fingers and anything they touch."

"It's called Chocolate Puppy Chow and happens to be Addy's favorite."

"That's just because it has an animal in the name." I pointed my egg yolk and mayo–covered knife at the sideboard where even more desserts waited on display. "You have stained-glass cookies and homemade s'more bars *and* Mexican wedding cookies, too."

"Weddin' cookies might come in handy if Zoe changes her mind about Reid wantin' to get hitched," Harvey said, laughing as Aunt Zoe grabbed a towel and swatted at him.

Mom slipped by them, stealing the towel from Aunt Zoe on the way to the sink. "I thought commitment was what you wanted from Reid the last time you were an item."

"Years ago, yes." Aunt Zoe uncovered Harvey's homemade rolls that had been left to rise and slid the tray into the top oven. "Now, it's a matter of fool me once, shame on him; fool me twice, shame on me."

I finished filling the remaining egg halves and tossed the knife into the dishwater. "But you asked him to marry you the first time, not the other way around."

"Reid really wants to settle down with you now. He seemed genuinely sincere." Mom grabbed a jar of olives from the refrigerator. "Doesn't that make a difference to you?"

A growl came from Aunt Zoe. "When it comes down to it, marriage is just a piece of paper. What matters is what's in his heart."

Harvey sprinkled fried onions on the top of the green bean casserole he'd thrown together earlier. "It doesn't hurt if he's rich enough to eat fried chicken every day, too."

"Don't let Elvis or Addy hear that," Mom said, playing along with a giggle. "Violet, get the sweet pickles out from the pantry, please."

"And the marshmallows," Aunt Zoe added.

"What also matters is what's in *your* heart," I said after I had a jar of homemade pickles in one hand and a bag of marshmallows in the other.

Aunt Zoe caught the bag when I tossed it to her. "I know what's going on in my ol' ticker. His? Not so much." She opened the bag and covered the casserole dish of yams with mini-marshmallows. "I thought I knew years ago, but he had the wool pulled over my eyes."

Harvey set the green bean casserole on the counter next to the stove. "You sure ya don't want to try trottin' along in a double harness for a bit? Single stalls get awful cold and lonely after a while, no matter how much straw you stuff all around ya. I know that for a fact."

"I'm positive," she said.

"If Sparky ends up moving in with Doc someday, a li'l company might be nice."

Moving in with Doc was something I'd thought about so many times while twiddling my thumbs at Calamity Jane Realty that I deserved the top spot on the Daydreamers Wall of Fame. However, I came with two kids, a cat, a hamster, and a chicken. While Doc enjoyed having me in his bed, I wasn't sure he'd be as thrilled about all of the fingerprints, cat hair, and chicken feathers that would result from our merging of abodes.

"I'll tell you what, Willis," Aunt Zoe said. "If Violet moves in with Doc, I'll save her room for you and your lazy ol' dog to keep me company in my lonely stall."

Harvey's grin hung from ear to ear. "Speaking on Ol' Red's behalf, it's a deal."

"Violet." Mom looked up from prepping the relish dish. "Go find Susan and have her help you set the table. The Christmas plates are in the china cabinet, along with some new cloth napkins I bought for the occasion."

I started to tell my mom I'd set the table on my own, but then remembered I was not going to cause any problems this Christmas. That vow included not bucking my mom at every turn when it came to Susan. "Okay. How much longer until we eat?"

"Probably about forty-five minutes, max," Aunt Zoe answered, getting a nod from Harvey.

"I'll let everyone know dinner is within the hour." I grabbed a handful of Chocolate Puppy Chow from the sideboard on my way out of the kitchen and shoved it all in my mouth at once. I needed all of the help I could get with being sweet when I ran into the holly-jolly harlot.

In the living room I found Layne standing in front of Cornelius, who lounged in my dad's recliner. My son was swinging his trident around in the air, slaying invisible enemies. I stood next to the Christmas tree, watching and listening.

"Who would you rather battle?" Layne took another swing. "Hydra or a kraken?"

"A kraken," Cornelius said without hesitation. "Hydra had poisonous breath and lethal blood."

"And if you chopped off one head, two would grow

back." Layne pretended to jab his enemy.

"Hydra's head regeneration is only in later versions of the story, of course."

"Of course," Layne parroted. "If you were walking alone at night in the middle of nowhere, would you rather come across a comozos in the Mexican jungle or a vampire in Transylvania?"

"Do you mean to say *Camazotz*, the creature that was periodically released from the Maya underworld to keep humans in line according to Maya mythology?"

"Yeah, that's the one. The giant demon thing with the head and wings of a bat but the body of a man. I read that he took out a whole village."

One of Cornelius's dark eyebrows rose. "Did you know that some experts believe Camazotz was based on a real creature?"

The trident lowered. "No way!"

"Yes way. Fossils were found in the Maya jungle of a giant bat that might have led to the myth."

Layne puffed out his chest. "I'd like to see a giant man-eating bat."

No, he wouldn't, but I kept my mouth shut. Layne was talking tough in front of Cornelius, trying to impress and bond with him. I'd seen Layne do the same thing with Cooper and Doc. My son was growing up, seeking out males as role models. I was lucky to have so many smart and strong examples to help teach Layne how to be a man worth his salt.

My eyes watered a bit as I watched Layne swing his trident again. I just prayed the lessons would help keep him alive when the monsters came.

Wait. That was negative. I thought of Camo-Claus's words and forced a smile to my lips. *Think positive thoughts.*

Okay. I was glad for these lessons because they would help keep Layne alive *if* the monsters came.

There. That was better.

I looked up to find Cornelius focused on me, his blue eyes searching. I smiled wider, willing the positivity to blaze forth.

He flinched and turned back to my son. "Layne, did you know that in China, people honor the bat as a good symbol for happiness and long life, especially if you see five in a group. They call it a five-fold blessing."

"Really?"

"Why five?" I asked, joining their conversation.

"The number five in Chinese traditions is considered very favorable to success. In this case, the five blessings were happiness, prosperity, longevity, luck, and wealth."

"How do you know all of this stuff about China and the Maya?" Layne asked.

"Cornelius loves to read," I explained.

"So do I." Layne's face lit up, his eyes big and round. He dropped onto the floor at Cornelius's feet, resting his trident in his lap. "What else do you know about bats?"

"Let's see." Cornelius stroked his pointy goatee. "In the realm of magic, bats are thought of as good for communication. If you build a bat house on your property, you can go call upon the bats to help you communicate better with other humans. My grandmother down in Louisiana had more than twenty bat houses on her farm."

"Wow!" Layne turned to me. "Can I build a bat house in Aunt Zoe's backyard?"

I shrugged. "You need to ask her that, not me."

Back to Cornelius, he said, "Did your grandma talk to the bats?"

"Wait," I interrupted. "Have either of you seen Susan?"

Layne pointed toward the door leading to the basement. "She didn't like us talking about slaying monsters on Christmas."

"Monster slaying isn't for everyone," I said.

Cornelius gave me one of his odd, crooked smiles. "Some have no choice in the matter."

That was a natural-born fact. I smiled back. "So, which one would you rather run into at night, Cornelius? Camazotz or Dracula?"

"Well, both are bloodsuckers, but I'd pick Dracula. He's easier to kill."

"How do you figure?" I asked.

"All I have to do is drag him out in the sun. According to legend, Camazotz is a far more dangerous foe."

I nodded. "Man-eating bat demons are deadly. Got it." With any luck, I'd not run into one any time soon.

I headed for the basement stairs. As I opened the basement door, I heard Layne ask, "Would you rather go out to dinner and a movie with a banshee or a siren?"

The familiar whistling music of one of my dad's favorite spaghetti westerns lured me downstairs.

When I was growing up, the basement was a rec room for us kids, somewhere my parents would send us to play so they could watch television in peace and quiet. As soon as all three of the kids had moved out, my dad took the space over as his game room, moving in a big-screen television, a high-tech stereo and sound system, a foosball table, a dartboard, and a mini-bar.

Over the years, he'd had to share it periodically, like with me when I moved back home now and then in need of my parents' help with raising my kids. Or like when Susan returned home months ago to regroup before flying back out into the world to suck the blood out of some other innocent soul.

Layne should have asked Cornelius if he'd rather face off with Susan in a dark alley or a giant man-eating bat.

I shook off my thoughts of Susan and her bloodsucking ilk and focused on Doc, who was waiting to take his turn at the dartboard. He'd showered while I was at the store with my mom, donning black jeans and a red flannel shirt for the holiday.

"Hey, good looking. Come here often?" I asked him as I crossed the rec room.

"Quiet, Parker," Cooper said while aiming his dart. "I'm trying to focus here."

Cooper had been the only one who hadn't brought a bag of clothes, since his plan had involved returning all of us to Deadwood in one piece. He wore his black henley shirt and blue jeans from yesterday that he'd washed and dried last night at the Morgan house.

A round of gunfire rattled from the speakers.

I smirked. "Like you can focus over the sound of Tuco and Blondie shooting up the town?"

"Gunplay is music to my ears," Cooper replied, closing one eye as he lined up his throw.

A glass clinked over at the minibar.

"Ohhhh," Susan purred. "I like a man who knows how to handle dangerous toys."

I grimaced, turning to look Medusa in the eye. Pillar of stone be damned.

Chapter Fifteen

Several remarks flew through my head while I held my tongue, none of them very Christmassy.

Stay positive, Violet, my mother's voice said in my head.

I smiled so hard it hurt. "Susan, why am I not surprised to find you down here with Doc and Cooper?"

"I came for the liquor." She held up a bottle of rum, and then leaned back against the bar, crossing her gazelle-like legs. "And stayed for the company."

I rolled my eyes at her stupid sexy-strumpet act. It wasn't an easy feat while holding that smile in place.

"Stop with that mad grin," she snapped. "You look like some kind of creepy clown who escaped the circus of the deranged."

I smiled even harder at her, making my eyes bulge.

"Come here, my little crazy clown." Doc caught my hand and pulled me to his side, kissing the smile off my lips.

"Miss me already?" I joked, tugging on both loose ends of the Gomez Addams tie looped around his neck. I'd found the tie online and hoped Doc wouldn't think it was too sappy of a gift. The smile and flirty wink he'd aimed my way when he'd opened it this morning had squelched my worries.

"Always, but that kiss was for good luck. Coop's on the verge of kicking my ass."

I chuckled, taking a step back from Doc. "What a coincidence. He's always on the verge of kicking mine."

Cooper threw the dart, missing the bull's-eye by a good inch. "Damn it, Parker. You're messing with my concentration."

"She's good at that," Doc said, scoping out the beaded v-neckline of my green tunic that I'd changed into after breakfast. "I haven't been able to think straight since July."

"Oh, look," Susan said, butting into our conversation. "A sprig of mistletoe." She dangled it out in front of her. "How fortunate that someone left it down here."

Crazy smile back in place, I strode over and snatched the mistletoe from her fingers.

"Hey!"

I stuffed it down the front of my black velvet leggings. "Not today, sister."

"Rude!" she said to my back as I walked away.

"How're things going in the kitchen?" Doc asked when I returned to his side and dropped the crazed smile.

"Aunt Zoe says dinner will be ready in about half an hour." I glanced at my sister, who was glaring daggers at me. The urge to flip her off came and went. Whew! I was getting good at this positivity shit. "Susan, Mom wanted me to tell you it's time to set the table."

She took a glass from the bar and poured two fingers of whiskey in it. "Why can't you set it?"

"Because I've been working in the kitchen."

"Maybe you should come help me anyway."

Frowning, I tried to figure out her angle. "Why would I want to do that?" Besides the fact that Mom said I was supposed to help her.

"Because it's our joint job to play hostess." She held up the glass of amber liquid. "Coop, here's your whiskey."

Coop? I mirrored Clint Eastwood's squint on the big screen. "Susan, be a good daughter and go set the table as your mother requested."

She set the glass of liquor down hard. "Take notice, Doc. Violet may seem sweet and innocent on the surface, but underneath that curly nest on her head she's a bossy bitch."

This time I did give her the finger, but I waited until her back was turned, so that had to be worth something on the character-building scale.

After she'd climbed the stairs, Doc chuckled and stepped up to the line to throw a dart. "Joke's on her. I knew you weren't sweet or innocent from the start."

"Really? You didn't buy my virtuous virgin routine?"

"Not with the way you looked at me when we were alone." He lined up the dart. "Not to mention the things you can do with those lips of yours."

Cooper groaned, grabbing the glass of whiskey Susan had poured for him. "Don't you two start with the lovey-dovey shit or I'll bury the next dart in your ass, Nyce."

Doc threw, his dart landing closer to the bull's-eye than Cooper's last one.

"Nice throw," I said, patting him on the butt.

"Parker, go back upstairs. You're ruining the game."

"Coop's a poor sport," Doc said. He caught my hand and lifted it to his lips. "Now, where were we, *cara mia*?"

"You were reminiscing about my lack of virtue."

"Right." His gaze lowered. "Did I or did I not see you stuff mistletoe down your pants a moment ago, gorgeous?"

Cooper cursed. "You two make me want to plant my head in a snow bank." He moved behind the bar. "Where's the ice? Your sister pours a lousy whiskey on the rocks."

Speaking of Susan, I scowled at Cooper. "You let my sister call you 'Coop' but not me?"

He smirked. "That's right."

I crossed my arms. "It's not very warm and fuzzy of you to be so mean to me on Christmas."

"I've told you before, I'm not a warm and fuzzy guy."

"He talks tough," Doc said, dropping my hand and lining up for another throw. "But I think he just needs some sugar to sweeten him up."

"Sugar, huh? Where is Natalie, anyway?" I goaded

Cooper, earning a glare in return. "Did you scare her away with your sharp and scratchy personality?"

Cooper flipped me off. Apparently, he needed to learn about the power of positivity. "She and Addy went outside to build a snowman."

I waited for Doc to throw his dart before asking, "What about Reid and my dad?"

"Reid offered to let your dad drive the snowcat," Doc explained, lining up his final throw. "They went for a ride."

"And you two let them? My dad wasn't packing when they left, was he?"

Cooper shrugged. "Martin will be fine. One bullet doesn't kill you."

It could in my world. "Not all of us are made of tin and missing a heart, Cooper."

"I have a heart."

"They issued it with his badge," Doc joked and threw his final dart. "Ha! Looks like you lose again, Coop."

"You suck, Nyce." He hit Doc with a rare grin. "How about three out of five?"

Doc turned to me. "Do you need our help with anything upstairs?"

"No, but thanks for asking." I gave him a peck on the cheek. "That's for more good luck. Now kick Cooper's whiny ass."

He grinned over at Cooper. "Will do, Killer."

I left the two of them to their testosterone-filled ribbing. Upstairs, I grabbed my new coat from the bedroom and headed for the front door. I passed Susan on the way. She had the plates set around the table and was collecting silverware from the china cabinet drawer.

"Violet," she said as I rushed past. "We need to talk."

That was never a good thing when it came to her. Talking quickly turned into bickering and that usually ended in yelling. "No time right now, Susan. I'm following Mom's orders."

"You're avoiding me."

"Don't think of it as avoiding," I said over my shoulder. "Think of it as pretending you're not here."

Outside, I found Dad and Reid standing beside the snowcat, hands in their coat pockets. The driveway and the road in front of our house were plowed clear for the moment, but the snow was still falling, albeit lighter than the last twenty-four hours.

"Hey, Goldilocks," Dad said as I approached them. "You remind me of your mom in that color."

Knowing what I did now about my father's appreciation for my mom and her yoga, I took that as a compliment and blocked any further thoughts about my parents in compromising positions. "Thanks. Did you plow or Reid?"

"Blake did," Reid answered. "He got the hang of driving the 'cat' pretty quickly."

My dad grinned like a boy with a new baseball and mitt.

"Good job, Pop," I said. "Mom wanted me to tell you we have about twenty minutes or so until dinner." I shaved off some time for my side trips on the way out here. "Have you heard from Quint today?"

"Not since last night."

"Neither has Mom. I wonder if he's on his way."

Reid looked up at the sky. "This storm isn't supposed to let up completely until late tonight. I'm not sure if the airport is even open."

I frowned, snuggling into my collar. Damn, it would be fun to see my brother again. We hadn't talked since Thanksgiving.

"Hey, knucklehead," Natalie called from the side of the house. "Come over here and check out your daughter's hard work."

I left the two big boys with their oversized toy and joined Natalie and Addy.

"Land sakes! You two have been busy." There was not one snowman, but two with twig arms, penny eyes, and stone smiles. "Where did you find the straw hat, lei, and grass skirt for the little one?"

Addy's cheeks and nose were pink when she looked up from adjusting the lei. "Nat brought them from her cousin's house. This snowman is like Grammy, all happy and dancing."

"Aunt Deborah had the accessories from when she had her big Hawaiian luau," Natalie said, scooping up a handful of snow. "It was the last family party she had before the divorce."

Oh, yeah. I remembered my mom's dress she'd bought for the party. "I love it—a snowman in paradise." I stepped closer to the bigger one. "I like the green scarf and matching hat. Are those your aunt's too?" They were pretty fancy for a snowman. I touched the fabric. "Is this cashmere?"

"We borrowed them from Aunt Susan," Addy answered, adjusting the matching cashmere hat.

I chuckled. "Does she know you borrowed them?"

"Not officially." Natalie scooped up more snow and

packed it onto the snowball she was forming. "It's going to be a surprise."

I laughed out loud at how Susan was going to react to her fancy hat and scarf wrapped around a snowman. "I love you, Natalie."

She blew me an air kiss.

"We wanted to make a snowman of each of the girls here," Addy said.

"So they could have a girls' night out after the sun sets," Natalie added.

"We need to make a snow chicken yet."

I blinked at my daughter. "A snow what?"

"Your daughter has poultry on the brain."

"Always." I glanced down at the snowball she was smoothing out. "Speaking of chickens, I just ran into a certain law dog down in the basement along with my sister, who was batting her eyelashes extra hard at him, if you know what I mean."

I pulled the sprig of mistletoe from my pants and handed it to Natalie.

She held it up in front of her. "What's that have to do with chickens?"

"Are you going to do anything about Cooper today or huddle in your safe little henhouse and cluck all night?"

She frowned at the mistletoe. "Why was this in your pants?"

"Don't change the subject. What are you going to do about your law dog?"

Her lips tightened. "He's not my law dog. If he wants to dally with your twisted sister, he can have at her."

I scoffed loud enough to make Addy jump and squeak. "You're so full of roasted chestnuts."

"Maybe, but it sounded tough, right?" She jammed the mistletoe sprig in the center of Susan the Snowwoman's forehead.

"It was totally weak. Are you out here avoiding him?"

"No." She lowered her voice for my ears only. "If you must know, Nosy Parker, I'm out here cooling down my libido. Did you see how good he looks in that black henley?"

I wrinkled my nose. "He looks like the same ol' snarly Detective Pissypants to me."

"Whatever." She pulled her arm back and launched the snowball. It hit Dad in the leg.

Dad looked over.

Natalie pointed at me.

He bent down and scooped up some snow. "Prepare to eat a snow-burger, Goldilocks!"

"No! Not my new coat." I screeched and dodged a snowball.

Addy squealed in delight and squished together a snowball, whipping it at her grandfather.

Ten minutes later, I tromped back inside the house, shaking the snow out of my hair. The table was set, and Susan was nowhere to be seen. She was probably back downstairs trying to sex up Cooper.

Slipping off my coat, I headed toward my bedroom. If I found out the Jolly Jezebel had laid one finger on Doc, I'd cram the kids' Christmas stockings down her throat, my vow not to ruin the day be damned.

I had company in my room. My favorite kind—tall, dark, and happy to see me.

Doc looked up from digging through his bag, his eyes dipping to my waist. "You still sporting that mistletoe, Vixen?"

"Why?" I hung my new coat in the closet. "You feel like doing some kissin', big boy?"

He grinned. "Something like that."

"What are you looking for?" I pointed at his bag.

"My phone charger." He pulled out a cord, coming over

to me. He plucked something from my hair. "Looks like you ran over the river and through the woods on the way to Grandmother's house."

"Natalie started a snowball fight with Dad and Reid. They bombarded us with snow bombs." I chuckled at the memory. "They make a good team."

"Your aunt won't be thrilled to hear that."

I walked over to the door and closed it. "While you're in here, I have something for you."

He rubbed his hands together. "Bring on that mistletoe."

"I left it outside."

"I'll improvise."

"My mother would like your positive attitude." I opened my dresser drawer and pulled out the present I had hidden under the linens my mom stored there. Now that the time had come to give him his last present, my heart was pounding hard. It had seemed like a good idea when the kids and I came up with it, but …

Before I could wimp out, I handed Doc the ten-by-ten inch box.

"What's this?"

I clasped my damp palms together. "One last present. This one is from the kids and me together."

His brow lifted. "Should I open it without them here?"

I nodded. If he didn't like the gift, I'd rather they not be here to see his face.

"Okay." He tore the paper off and pulled off the box lid, staring down at the gift for one second less than an eternity. When he looked up, his expression was hard to decipher.

My gut flip-flopped. "I hope you don't mind," I said hurriedly as he set it down on the bed, my voice sounding fluttery. "The kids and I thought you might like it for your desk at work, but if it makes you uncomfortable, I can tell them—"

He grabbed me by the shoulders and kissed me with an intensity that consumed every single thought rattling around in my head. When he pulled back, I had to blink a couple of times in order to touch back down on Earth.

"Does that mean you like it?" I whispered.

He picked the gift up again, smiling at the picture frame Addy and Layne had decorated together. "I love it."

Doc's name was scrawled across the top of the frame in Addy's best writing. She'd added a puffy chicken sticker after his name. Layne had drawn an orange dragon along the bottom.

Inside the frame was a picture of the kids and me that Aunt Zoe had taken last summer in her backyard. It wasn't one of my better shots. My hair was spiraling half out of my ponytail and my makeup was sparse, but the three of us were giggling about something, so the photo showed the real deal. The kids had insisted it was one of our best pictures, so I'd consented.

"They both made you homemade cards, too." I pointed at the envelope that had been under the frame. It held both cards.

He pulled out Addy's first. On the front was a drawing of a blond stick girl and a stick chicken wearing a sweater. Inside, she'd written how much she loved Doc's French toast and how happy she was that he liked her mother.

Chuckling, he lowered the card. "Wooed by food. Like mother like daughter."

"We're easy that way."

He set Addy's card aside and opened Layne's.

My son had drawn a sword that looked like one of the weapons from his medieval books. Inside, he'd written something that he'd refused to let me see at the time.

"What's it say?" I asked, leaning closer. "Layne wouldn't let me read it."

Doc handed me the card. "Your kids are tough on a lonely bachelor's heart."

I looked down at the card, reading Layne's scrawls:

My mom told me that you don't have a mom anymore, so when you're sick or scared or lonely you have nobody to hug you and make you feel better. Since you need a mom and I have a good-smelling one who likes to hug, I will share her with you.

P.S.—Watch out when you have sleepovers with my mom. She has very cold feet and kicks a lot.

P.S.S.—Addy kicks a lot, too.

I looked up at Doc, swiping the tears from my eyes. "Good thing for you I don't stink, huh?"

He pulled me into his arms, wrapping me in a tight hug. "Thank you, Violet."

"That gift was partly the kids' idea."

He tipped my chin up. "I mean thank you for giving me a wonderful Christmas with your family."

My heart swelled at the love in his dark eyes. "Don't jinx us, Candy Cane. The day isn't over yet."

"Violet! Doc!" Aunt Zoe called. "It's time to eat."

Doc followed me out into the dining room. Everyone else was in the process of sitting down at the table while licking their chops and complimenting the cooks. Doc whispered something in Addy's ear and then Layne's, leaving each of them with big grins, before taking the chair next to me.

We'd all settled in at the table with the food steaming in front of us when the doorbell rang.

I looked at Dad. "Quint?"

He frowned toward the front door. "He doesn't usually ring the bell, but maybe his arms are full." He started to get up, but I beat him to the punch.

"I'm closer. I'll get it." I jogged to the door, my heart pounding with excitement at seeing my brother again.

"It's about time," I said as I opened the door.

It wasn't Quint.

A short, round man with a walrus mustache and one of those furry Russian winter hats was waiting on the porch.

"Uh … can I help you?"

He stared at me for a second, inspecting me from top to bottom. "I'm looking for Violet Parker." His voice reminded me of Burl Ives's when he narrated *Rudolph the Red-Nosed Reindeer.*

"I'm Violet."

"Great!" His mustache curved upward at the corners. "You're a hard woman to find."

"I am?"

He held out an envelope for me to take.

After a moment's hesitation, I grabbed it. My name was written on the front. "What's this?"

"A letter from your attorney."

"*My* attorney?" What attorney?

"That's what I was told when I was hired to find you and deliver it in person."

I tried to process his words, but I hit a wall. "Why were you hired to find me?"

His mustache dipped into an upside-down horseshoe. "I'm afraid I have bad news."

"You do?"

His expression grew somber. "Your husband is dead."

Chapter Sixteen

*M*y husband?"

The guy pointed a pudgy finger at the envelope in my hand. "I was told it's all explained in there for you."

The gears in my brain ground on his words. In particular, it was still trying to make sense of the word *husband*. Was this something to do with Rex and his attempt to blackmail me into playing "family" with him so he could land that stupid job promotion? But why would he play dead?

"You're a widow," he added, as if that cleared up everything for me.

It didn't. Not even a teeny-tiny bit.

I stuffed the envelope inside the front of his coat.

"Nope." I rejected him and his envelope.

"What? Wait!" he said as I shut the door in his face.

"Violet?" Dad called from the other room.

I looked toward the dining room. My left eye started twitching.

I had a husband.

A dead husband.

How had I managed that? Shouldn't I remember getting married? Had there been tequila involved?

I turned back to the front door. Was I dreaming?

I opened the door again.

The round man with the furry Russian hat still stood there. He smiled, his walrus moustache curving with his cheeks. "Hi again." He held up the envelope. "You want this back?"

Not really, but I took the envelope anyway. "Who are

you again?"

"A private investigator hired to find Violet Parker."

Nope, this wasn't Rex. He knew where I lived.

I looked down at the envelope with my name on it. "I think you have the wrong Violet Parker."

He flipped open a notepad and held it up for me to see. "Is that your Social Security number?"

"Yes."

"Then I have the right Violet Parker." His gaze measured me up and down. "Although I thought you'd be taller from the description I was given. And brunette."

Tall and brunette?

An inferno erupted in my chest.

Susan!

What had the two-bit trollop done now?

The flames spread to my fingers and toes with wildfire speed. I could almost feel the smoke billowing from my ears as the blaze moved north.

"Violet?" Mom called this time. "Who's at the door?"

On the verge of spontaneous combustion, I tried to find something positive to focus on to cool my core before I hit nuclear meltdown mode. What was that old Elvis quote Aunt Zoe liked to say? Something about when things went wrong in life, find the bitch responsible and bury her six foot under in the backyard?

No, that wasn't it.

Ah, screw it. I was going to have to improvise.

"Have you had Christmas dinner?" I asked the short version of Magnum, P.I.

"Uh, no. Are you okay?" He pointed at my face. "Your left eye looks a little buggered up."

"It's quite possible I'm having a stroke." I grabbed him by the shoulder and hauled him inside the foyer. "Why don't you join us at the table? We're getting ready to eat."

"I ... well ... I don't think ... I mean ..." He wiped his

boots on the doormat.

"Great. Let's get this off of you." I tossed his furry hat over my shoulder. "We'll be right there," I hollered to my parents.

"Listen, lady. I really don't think—"

"Neither does my sister," I said in a terse whisper. "She acts on her emotions." I unbuttoned his coat. "My mom explained it all to me at the minimart earlier."

"She did?" He frowned behind his big mustache as I tugged his coat off his shoulders.

"And while I'd like to fill my sister's head with cannon balls and powder her behind," I continued, echoing Johnny Horton's line from "The Battle of New Orleans," "Mom says Susan needs our love and support." I wadded his coat into a ball and stuffed it under the shoe bench, kicking it once for good measure.

He shot a worried glance at his coat and then back at me. "Love and support are always good things."

"You'd think so, but here you are with that envelope." I smiled extra wide, stretching my whole face to fit it all in.

He cringed. "You could scare children with that face."

"Wonderful. Let's go eat." I grabbed his wrist and dragged him into the dining room.

Upon arrival, all eyes focused on me and my new guest.

"Hello, everyone. I'd like you to meet Mr. …" I turned to him. "I'm sorry, I didn't get your name?"

"Peabody. Norman D. Peabody."

"Norman D. Peabody it is. He's a private investigator who's come bearing sad news on this joyous day."

"Violet," Mom said, half-rising, her expression lined with concern. "You're frightening me with that face. Please stop smiling."

"I'm just trying to remain positive, Mother. Nobody likes a Negative Nelly, especially on Christmas."

Dad caught my mom's hand and pulled her back to her

seat. His expression matched Mom's. "What sad news, Goldilocks?"

I held up the envelope with my name and focused on my sister. "Apparently, my husband has died."

To her credit, Susan didn't even flinch.

My mother, on the other hand, swooned. She would have fallen out of her chair if Dad hadn't caught her. She'd definitely earn an Emmy at this year's awards ceremony for Outstanding Guest Performer in a Drama Series.

It took a second—or five—for everyone else to pick their jaws up off the table.

"Husband?" Aunt Zoe repeated. Apparently, she was struggling with that word the same as I had.

"Holy wedlock!" Harvey said through a mouthful of dinner roll.

"When did Mom get married?" Addy asked her brother.

Layne frowned at me. "Was he our real dad?"

"Is this some kind of practical joke?" Natalie looked back and forth between Peabody and me and then toward the front door. "Is Quint hiding in the foyer?"

"It's no joke," Mr. Peabody said. "I've been trying to get hold of Violet Parker for a couple of weeks, but she wouldn't return my calls from the number listed or reply to my letters sent to the post office box I'd been given. I figured Christmas Day would be my best chance to catch her in person at her parents' known address."

"And he was right." I shot Cooper a smirk. "Maybe the Deadwood Police Department should hire him to replace your barking partner."

Reid crossed his arms. "What's the cause of death?"

Good question. I hadn't even gotten that far yet what with still trying to digest that I had somehow gotten married.

"I hope you have an alibi for this one, Parker," Cooper said, aiming a smirk right back at me.

"This can't be happening," my mom said, her voice wavering.

"Denial is the first stage of grief," Cornelius pointed out. "Will somebody pass me the mushroom caps?"

"Oh, hell. Here we go again." Dad pushed away from the table. "Anyone else need a drink?"

"Violet." Doc stood and pulled out my chair. "Maybe you should come sit down."

I shook my head at him. There was no way I could think about eating at the moment with the way my gut was burning. It was all I could do not to open my mouth and blast my sister with a fireball of rage. "If you all would please make our guest feel welcome, I'd appreciate it. You know, 'tis the season and all that Christmas spirit shit."

Before I said something I'd regret later, I left the room and made a beeline for the front door, grabbing my snow boots on the way. I didn't even bother with a coat. I was so hot under the collar that I'd probably melt all of the snow in a one-block radius.

Once outside, I tore open the envelope and scanned the contents. My hands trembled as I read, and then my vision turned red. Huffing like I was heading into labor, I looked up and saw the snowwoman Addy had made decorated with Susan's scarf and hat.

"Perfect!"

After yanking on my boots, I grabbed the snow shovel from where it leaned against the porch railing and tromped across the yard.

How could she? Married in *my* name, hiding behind *my* fucking Social Security number.

I wanted to kill her.

No, wait. Death would be too quick. Maiming would be better after several rounds of torture first.

With a growl at the sky, I raised the snow shovel and swung, knocking the snowman's head clear off in one blow.

Susan's hat went with it. The second blow took a big chunk out of the chest cavity. The third finished the job on the middle.

When I raised the shovel for a fourth whack at it, someone grabbed the handle.

"Violet!" Doc's voice cut through my raging torrent of cursing. "Stop!"

I turned, my breath coming hard and fast. "She …" I swallowed a blazing ball of fury. "She stole my identity and married some guy." I let him take the shovel from me. "*Married*, Doc. What kind of twisted, mentally fucked-up person does that to her own flesh and blood?"

He buried the shovelhead in the snow.

I covered my face with my cold palms, dragging my fingers down my cheeks. "I feel so … so … so violated."

Without saying a word, Doc wrapped his coat around my shoulders and pulled me into his arms.

I bounced my forehead against his sternum, wishing I could snap my fingers and make this mess go away. "I knew she was up to something. Mom said I was just being a pessimist again and looking for problems where none existed, but I knew deep in my gut."

"Susan came clean to your parents after you left," he said, stroking my hair. "Your mom left the table in tears. Your dad is consoling her in their room."

Turning my head, I rested my cheek against his warm chest and listened to the steady beat of his heart. "Are the kids okay?"

"They're confused, but Natalie is helping them understand the situation."

"What about everyone else?"

"Harvey told them to eat while the food was hot, so they are, including Mr. Peabody."

"Good. I didn't want to ruin Christmas."

His chest vibrated. "I think your sister took the top

prize for that today, sweetheart. But your daughter might be a bit hurt about the damage you inflicted on her poor snowman."

I leaned back and looked at the aftermath of my storm of rage. All that was left was the bottom ball. Susan's scarf was half-buried under the snow. I grimaced. "Good thing snowmen don't bleed."

"Remind me never to piss you off when there's a shovel within reach."

I turned back to him. "What am I going to do, Doc?"

He blew out a breath. "One way or another, we're going to figure out how to unravel you from this spider web."

"I could go to the police and claim identity fraud, but that hurts my parents more than Susan." I didn't even want to think about how much of a mess this would be with the IRS.

"Lucky for you, we know a certain detective who might be able to give us some advice on where to start."

"Oh, God." I groaned and dropped onto the bottom of the annihilated snowman. "This is so embarrassing."

"You shouldn't feel embarrassed, sweetheart. You did nothing wrong."

"Yes, I did. I dragged everyone inside of that house into my sordid family drama. I'm sure witnessing the mushroom cloud spurred by my non-wedding to a complete stranger is *not* how they wanted to spend their holiday."

He squatted in front of me, holding my knees. "Violet, you need to understand something about the people in that house. They are your family. Some may not be related by blood, but they would put their lives on the line to help you just the same. Hell, most of them already have in one way or another over the last few months." When I frowned in the direction of my parents' place, he added, "Even Cooper."

Doc was right. I was fortunate to have each and every

one of them by my side. But I wasn't going to admit that to Cooper unless he said it first.

I looked down at my palms. They were red from the cold. I covered his hands with mine. "And what about you?"

"What about me?"

I met his dark eyes. "I'm spoiled goods."

"What are you talking about?"

"This could get ugly, Doc. There's a will. That's why Mr. Peabody had to find me. There's money involved here. Susan didn't marry some beach bum down in the Caribbean. She found herself a rich old guy and apparently convinced him to add her—or rather me—to his will."

"How much money are we talking about?"

"Enough that the lawyer hired a private investigator to hunt me down."

He cursed under his breath.

"Exactly. I don't want to drag you into this."

His gaze narrowed. "It's not your choice, it's mine."

"Yeah, but—"

"Listen, Killer. I'm not sure if you've been taking notes, but you and I are a team. Where you go, I go. When you fight, I fight. Nothing short of death is going to change that between us."

His words made my heart thud hard against my ribcage. I laced my fingers with his. "As in 'til death do us part?" I jested. Sort of.

A grin crept onto his face. "Even after death if I go first, because I'm coming back to haunt you."

"Deal." I sighed, easing some of the pressure in my chest. "I wonder how long I've been married to this guy."

He stood and plucked the sprig of mistletoe from the broken pieces of the head, pocketing it. "I wonder how long I've been fooling around with a married woman."

A married woman. That was me, only the guy was all

wrong. I groaned. "Criminy. Why me? Why couldn't Susan use her own damned identity?"

He held out his hand. "Let's go find out."

I took it. "Doc?"

"Yeah?"

"Thank you for coming after me."

He pulled me to my feet. "For you, *cara mia*, I'd ride a tornado bareback."

I laughed, still holding his hand. "Ah, Gomez. You're dearer to me than all of the bats in all of the caves in the world," I said, quoting Morticia Addams. Make that all of the bats except for the giant man-eating kind. Those I'd leave for Cornelius to handle.

Doc squeezed my cold knuckles. "Prove it, Killer." Hooking his arm around my shoulders, he led me toward the house.

Chapter Seventeen

Other than a dead husband, Christmas dinner went off without a hitch.

Upon my return from beating the hell out of Addy's snowman, I learned that Susan had escaped to her room in the basement, which left the table full of my "family." Well, except for Mr. Peabody, but he fit right in, bantering with Cornelius, who appeared to be vetting him to find some ghosts that had gone missing.

My parents came back midway through the meal. My mom graced us all with a smile. "I apologize for my emotional outburst. It's not every day that my little girl gets married."

That surprised a laugh out of me. Several others, too.

"Hell," Dad added, "I always thought Violet's wedding would drain my bank account." He raised his glass in my direction. "Thanks for saving me money, Goldilocks. I only wish I could have been there to walk you down the aisle."

I raised my glass in return. "I wish I'd been there, too." I would have run fast and far the other way.

By the time the dishes were cleared and the multitude of pies and other desserts were brought to the table, I was ready to find out the exact depth of Susan's betrayal. I excused myself from the table, squeezing Doc's shoulder when he looked up at me.

"I'll be back in a bit," I told him.

"Violet?" My mother's brow furrowed. "Where are you going?"

She knew where I was heading. "I'll be good, Mom. I promise."

"Do you want help?" she asked.

"No, thanks. This is something I need to do alone."

I grabbed two plates, loaded them with cherry pie, and headed downstairs.

Susan didn't answer on the first knock, but I heard something thump on the other side of the door.

"I know you're in there. You might have a skinny ass, but it's not small enough to squeeze through the window."

The lock clicked and the door opened.

Susan had changed into a black sweater and leggings, reminding me of a black widow spider with her long, thin limbs. She was twice as deadly, I knew for a fact.

I held out the pie. "I brought you a piece of your favorite." I glanced down at her gazelle body. "That is, if you eat anything besides grass these days."

She eyed the pie suspiciously. "Did you poison it?"

I harrumphed. "I thought about it, but Mom hid the hemlock from me."

"Thanks." She took the plate and stood back, making room for me to enter.

I stepped into her lair, noting the open luggage on her bed. "You going somewhere?"

She shrugged and dug her fork into the pie. "I've worn out my welcome here."

That was one way of putting it. "Heading any place in particular?"

"Maybe."

I didn't blame her for holding her cards close to her vest. I always did around her. "I hear the moon has a few openings, but we might need to weigh you down so you don't float back to Earth."

"Funny," she said with a straight face.

Moving to the dresser, I leaned against it and took a bite of pie. I had a feeling I'd need every last sweet crumb to keep my bitterness at bay. "So, who was he?" When she looked at me with her perfectly shaped eyebrows arched, I added, "The man *we* married."

She set her plate down on the bookshelf full of our childhood favorites. I shoved another piece of pie in my mouth as she crossed the room and stared out the narrow basement window.

"Hey." She leaned closer to the glass, scowling. "Is that my scarf out there in the snow?"

And her hat, too. "We'll have to ask Frosty later."

She hit me with a glare. "That's an expensive scarf."

I smiled, my positivity gushing. "That's too bad. Now quit stalling and tell me about our husband."

She crossed her arms. "He was rich."

"I figured that based on the amount of money he left us according to the letter."

"And alone."

That made sense, too. Why else would he have left gobs of cash to a woman hiding behind a false identity?

"Did you love him?" I asked.

She scoffed. "There's only been one man I loved."

Right, Rex. I gagged a little on Mom's pie. What Susan saw in that pompous prick was beyond me. Sure, he was handsome, but below the surface everything was slimy and bloated, oozing with maggots.

"Why did you do it?"

"Do what?" She gave me a brittle smile. "Marry him or use your identity?"

"Both."

"Why not?" she said, hiding behind flippancy.

"Don't play games with me, Susan. Not here, not now. It's just the two of us, and I deserve answers."

With an exaggerated sigh, she left the window and dropped onto the edge of the bed. "Back in May, I met a man in an airport bar. I was on my way to Florida for a job with a gallery down in Key West. He was waiting for a flight to go meet with a client in St. Barts."

"That's an island in the Caribbean, right?"

She nodded. "We spent an interesting few hours during our layovers."

I tried extra hard not to roll my eyes. "You had wild monkey sex, I get it."

"Actually, we didn't. There was some flirting, but we spent the time talking about our jobs. He was an attorney who specialized in estate taxes. The conversation was actually quite mundane. Shortly before it was time for him to board, he gave me his business card and told me that if the Florida job didn't work out and I was interested in earning a lot of money in a short time, to give him a call."

"And you believed him?"

"No, of course not. I went to Key West, but within a week, I was bored out of my mind. One night, after a couple of drinks, I found his number in my purse. When I called, he told me the job was still available and offered to pay for my flight down to St. Barts."

"Let me guess. High-paid call girl?"

She tried to look offended, but I wasn't buying it. "I asked if sex was involved and he said he didn't think it would be necessary to seal the deal, but that I needed to bring some of my more alluring outfits and a fake identity."

A Caribbean island, an estate lawyer, quick money. All of this seemed so unreal. Like something out of a James Bond movie. "Why *my* name?"

"I didn't have time to get a fake ID. I knew your details, including your Social Security number from when you had it taped to your wall in your bedroom."

I'd been sixteen at the time and trying to memorize it for job applications.

"To be honest, I never figured this so-called job of his would amount to much, or I would have chosen a better cover than hiding behind you."

"I wish you had. What happened next?"

"The lawyer met me at the airport, took me shopping at some very pricey boutiques, and then dropped me off at a hotel, promising to return to take me to dinner in the evening. Later, I dressed the part and dined with him at a posh club. During the meal, he took me over and introduced me to one of his clients, an old man who was eating alone. Only instead of claiming I was his date, he said I was his sister and had come down there to heal after losing my husband to a long, ugly battle with lung cancer."

She shifted, crossing her legs on the bed as though she was practicing yoga. "I caught onto the game and within the hour was sharing drinks with the old guy in the club bar, listening to him go on and on about his life." She groaned. "And trust me, Hooch could talk about himself until my ears bled."

"Hooch? That's the name of the man we married?" It sounded like something Harvey would name a dog.

"It was his nickname. His real name was Herman Oleander Osmond Winchester, Jr., but he preferred Hooch for short."

Okay, Hooch it was. "Was the lawyer there with you?"

"No, he left us so we could get to know each other. The next night, I went to dinner with Hooch on my own. This went on for over a week, me flirting and listening to the old geezer drone about his long life—he was ninety-two, so he had plenty of boring stories to tell. By the end of the week, I'd learned two things—Hooch was lonely for a companion and he had lung cancer, same as my fictitious dead husband."

I moved over to the dressing chair, pushed her clothes aside, and settled in to see how this tale ended up with Mr. Peabody showing up on our doorstep on Christmas Day. "So, how long did it take for Hooch to change his will?"

"I spent the rest of May and all of June and July wooing

him."

"Did you end up screwing him?"

She smirked. "No, Hooch only liked to watch while I took care of myself. He was long past being able to get a full erection."

Grimacing, I tried to forget that detail before it took up residence in my brain and registered for a post office box. "That's too much information, Susan."

"You're the one who asked."

Lesson learned. "What about the lawyer?"

"Oh, he could still get it up and was rather large in the briefs. He probably had a good inch on Rex. We screwed around during Hooch's naptimes, but we had to be sneaky. There were tons of cameras around the house. Like I said, he was into watching."

I squeezed the bridge of my nose. The last thing I wanted to reminisce about on Christmas Day was Rex Conner's nether regions. "I meant, what did the lawyer get out of you wooing Hooch?"

"If you want specific answers, then you need to improve your interrogation skills."

"Duly noted."

"The lawyer and I convinced Hooch to make him the executor of his estate with full access to all of his accounts."

"And whose idea was it to include you in the will?"

"Hooch thought it was his."

"But your lawyer pal was whispering in Hooch's ear about your innumerable qualities, I'm sure."

She lifted her chin at my backhanded insult. "I was a poor widow with a broken heart and two children to raise. The money would keep me and my kids off the streets."

Errrch! Back the truck up. "Two children?"

She leaned back on the heels of her palms. "As you know, Violet Parker has two kids, so of course I had adorable twins whose pictures I kept next to our bed."

"Your and Hooch's bed?"

"Yes."

"My kids' pictures sat next to a strange old man's bed?"

"A rich old man."

As much as I wanted to throttle her, I laced my fingers together and let her continue. "So, the will was changed, the lawyer became the executor, and you were added as a beneficiary."

"Me and my kids."

Come again? "The letter only mentioned me."

"The new will split his estate into fourths. One part to a grant program at his alma mater; another part to his only living relative—some adopted nephew he hadn't seen in almost thirty years; a third part to Violet Parker; and the final fourth to Violet Parker's kids, split evenly, of course."

Nutcracker balls! This was even worse than I'd thought. "Okay, so the will was changed and then what? You kicked back on the beach and waited for him to die?"

"Yeah, pretty much. The cancer had spread throughout his body and by early July he was sleeping most of the day and night. I made sure the nurses changed him routinely and rolled him over so the bedsores didn't get any worse. But the old bastard would not die."

How horrible to be in such a wretched state and surrounded by gold-digging vultures.

"Don't give me that look, Violet. You don't understand. Hooch wasn't a kind and compassionate man in his youth. He was a ruthless, cutthroat businessman who took great pleasure in hostile takeovers that ended with him squeezing all of the value from his acquisitions before squishing them under his heel like bugs."

"You're just saying that to make yourself feel better."

"It's the truth. He told me tale after tale about how he destroyed so many lives, grinning the whole time with glee as he bragged about his might in the business world." She scoffed. "Do you actually think I would do this to some innocent old guy?"

Yes! Wait, let me think about that for a moment … Hell yes! Instead of answering her, I asked, "How come you ran off instead of waiting for Hooch to die?"

She wrinkled her upper lip. "Well, I got into some trouble with the lawyer."

"What kind of trouble?"

"The love kind."

"What does that mean?"

"He fell in love with me—or so he claimed."

I sneered. "He just wanted the money Hooch was giving you and the kids."

"I thought so, too, at first. But it got weird."

"Define 'weird.' "

She stood and began pacing at the end of the bed. "He'd buy me jewelry, bring me roses, talk about adopting your kids as his own. He even got a tattoo of my profile over his heart with 'Violet' written under it."

"Why my name? He knew your real name, didn't he?"

"Yes, but when we screwed around, he'd call me by your name. He said it made our dirty romps more exciting."

I covered my mouth. Oh, my poor sullied name.

"I soon realized that I was trapped," Susan continued, still pacing. "If I came clean about my true identity to Hooch, I'd lose out on the money." She frowned down at her hands. "And by that point I'd done some things to get your name on that will that went beyond deranged. Hooch had kinky tastes, trust me. Money can make people really unbalanced."

I wasn't even going to fish in that murky pond. "It sounds like the lawyer played you."

"He had dreams of us living on the island in Hooch's house, raising your kids—even though he knew they weren't mine—and growing old together there."

"So you ran." My tone overflowed with derision.

She stopped pacing and scowled at me. "I didn't know what else to do. I figured that if I disappeared, Hooch would realize I didn't love him and change his will again."

"What about all of those gross kinky things you did?"

"Well, you see, there was this guy I'd met at the clubhouse. He owned a local upscale art gallery."

"You've got to be fucking kidding me. You were having sex with him, too?"

She slapped her hands on her hips. "I didn't have sex with him. I just agreed to help him with a couple of shows."

"Fine. You helped him. What's that have to do with this whole sordid mess?"

"I realized during those shows that I was much happier surrounded by art, and that my dream was to open my own gallery."

Golly gee, I was certainly glad that I could play a part in Susan finding her dream career. Now I could go to my deathbed feeling fulfilled.

"The weight of that stupid will started to make it hard to breathe." She returned to wearing out the carpet. "After another couple of weeks I'd had enough. I snuck away and took a flight back to the States."

"But what about the money you'd sleazed so hard for?"

Her eyes narrowed. "In exchange for a few disgusting moments with Hooch, I'd enjoyed living a life of luxury in his huge beach house for months. That was good enough for me by that point. End of story."

"But it's not the end of the story, is it?"

"No." She blew out a breath. "Unfortunately, Hooch didn't change his will and the fool lawyer was still pining over me. I'd given a fake address back in the States on all of the paperwork I'd signed, which kept him at bay until two weeks ago. He'd tracked down my last address and sent me a letter, which the post office forwarded to me here. In it, he explained that Hooch had died in November and I was still in the will. He also sent me several love poems he'd written since I'd left." She wrinkled her nose. "He's still using your name in them."

This whole story was nutty as peanut butter frosted fruitcake. "Is that all?" I asked.

"No, he also sent me a picture of his penis. You should see it. Even you'd be impressed."

I flinched. "I meant, is that all of your story about how I ended up married to a man I never knew existed?"

"Yeah. That's it."

I sat there for a moment, letting it all gel in my head. "What did I wear at my wedding?"

"A sexy little nurse uniform with fishnet stockings and a pair of Valentino Garavani rockstud ankle-strap heels. Hooch really got off when I played Violet the slutty nurse with him and took his temperature with my extra-long thermometer."

Eek! I was going to need to soak my brain in bleach for a month to clear these stains. "Well, at least I was wearing nice shoes." I covered my face with my hands, peering at Susan through my fingers. "What did I ever do to you?"

"Besides the obvious?"

"What's the obvious?"

She pointed at me. "You treated me differently."

I lowered my hands. "Different from what?"

"From Quint. I could never quite put my finger on it until you came clean about Blake not being my real dad."

"He raised you as his own."

"Yes, he did, but you didn't treat me like a sibling."

"What in the hell are you talking about?"

"When you looked at Quint, your eyes practically glowed with adoration. Then you'd turn to me and there was nothing there but hate."

Not hate. Not at first, anyway. "That's because you kept

destroying my things."

"I only did that because I was mad at you for not adoring me like you did Quint."

Dear Lord in a flatbed Ford! My sister was driving on one lug nut.

"Is that why you screwed Rex? Because I didn't adore you enough growing up?"

"I fell in love with Rex," she defended.

Apparently, my mom had been telling the truth on that one. "How could you fall in love with someone you barely knew?"

"Barely knew?" She sniffed. "Rex and I were having sex long before the day you caught us."

"What?"

She looked like the cat that had eaten the canary. "I guess Rex never told you about that and how we'd—"

"Stop!" I held up my hand. "So, you and Rex were screwing around behind my back before the day I caught you two in my bed?"

"Yes. We'd had sex in your bed several times before that day."

I let that settle in my gut, waiting for the flames of anger to flare. Oddly, I felt nothing—no ire, no hurt, no humiliation. Hmmm, that was different.

"Rex liked to keep our rendezvous hush-hush. He said it made him hot thinking about me as his naughty secret."

Of course. Rex had been into all kinds of stupid sex games. I'd donned a few silly getups myself back then upon request. Memories flashed through my mind, my cheeks warming at my stupid naiveté. Ah, there was my old friend, humiliation. Welcome back.

I returned to Susan and the here and now. "And you fell in love with him?"

"Yes."

"You didn't think him screwing around with you behind

my back was a red flag when it came to a long-term relationship with the rat bastard?"

"Rex told me he loved me. That he was going to break it off with you, but he wanted to let you down easy."

That dickhead had been playing both of us.

"Enough about Rex." I stood from the chair. "You need to fix this mess with the will."

"That's what Mom said, too." She rubbed the back of her neck. "I made her cry."

I held back a snort. Hell, I'd made our mom cry more times than I could remember. She'd bawled buckets when I told her I was pregnant. What surprised me was that causing Mom's tears seemed to bother Susan all of a sudden. Apparently even black widows have hearts.

I looked at her luggage. "Are you running away again?"

"I'm going back to St. Barts."

"Why?"

"Mom told me I have to make things right by you."

Hmm. Susan's history when it came to anything involving me raised some doubts. How could I trust that she wouldn't go and screw up things even more?

But before we went any further, I wanted to address something else. "You need to keep your hands off of Doc."

She rolled her eyes. "Hold your breath. I saw him with the kids this morning while they were playing with their presents. I'm not going near that."

"And I'm supposed to believe you after your past with my boyfriends?"

"Those other guys were ticking time bombs. I'm surprised you couldn't see it." She glanced at my hair. "Then again, you were always an easy mark for charmers, falling for anyone spewing compliments about your curls."

I let that blast about my hair fly over my bow. "And you were merely helping me out by sleeping with them?"

She shrugged. "If they hadn't shown interest, I would've

backed off. But you kept choosing two-timing losers. What was I supposed to do? Let my sister be the butt of their locker room jokes?"

"Please! You took pleasure in screwing them behind my back. Don't even try to deny it."

"Pleasure? Other than Rex, one of them was okay in the sack. Another was like a monkey. He went off before he even got it out of his pants."

"Wait a second! How many of my boyfriends did you sleep with?" Before she could answer, I held up my hand again. "You know what? Never mind. It doesn't matter. My point was, you took pleasure in hurting me."

"Didn't we already go over this? Must we beat it into the ground?"

I'd like to beat her into the ground with a big ol' ... I clasped my hands together, looking at her luggage again. An idea popped into my head. Insurance, of sorts, that she'd clean up this mess. "Let's make a deal, Susan."

"Why would I be interested in a deal with you?"

I ignored her sarcasm. "If you get me and my kids out of this mess, free and clear, I'll help you lure Rex back." All I had to do was get him onto her sticky web and then she could scuttle in and immobilize him with a bite or two.

Her gaze narrowed. "Why would you do that?"

Because I wanted to kill two birds with one stone. A big stone that was strapped to the end of my new mace. A pointy stone would be best. Unfortunately, Cooper insisted that murder would get me jail time, so I'd have to settle for manipulating Susan and Rex into leaving the Black Hills of their own free will.

I smiled, my positivity shining like a beacon through the shitstorm. At least, that was the look I was trying to fake. "Just call me a sucker for true love."

Chapter Eighteen

What was it about Christmas lights that made everything in life seem okay? Or maybe it was what the lights represented for me—comfort food, shared laughs, and family … including the ornery law dog across the puzzle table from me.

"Quit looking at me with that goofy grin, Parker."

"Come on, Cooper." I looked down at the puzzle pieces, searching for one with part of a green stocking. "Can't we just put away our fangs for one night? It's Christmas, for Pete's sake."

And Susan has left the state.

Earlier, after our little talk, Susan had finished packing and caught a ride south to Denver with Mr. Peabody, who lived down near Colorado Springs. According to Mr. Peabody, the storm had stayed north and the roads were mostly clear a little ways south of Rapid City. The Denver airport was Susan's best bet with Rapid's airport not only still closed, but also backed up from cancelled flights.

Mom and Dad had seen her off. I figured she and I had said enough to each other down in the basement. She knew the deal—one "fuckup" for another, as in her dissolving "my" bogus marriage in exchange for me manipulating Rex into her hands.

Later in the afternoon, Doc and the kids had gone outside to play in the snow, staying out so long that I'd donned my old coat and gone out to see what they were up to. I found them in the side yard, along with a couple more new snowmen.

I stopped short at the sight of Addy battling one of the

snowmen with my old softball bat. She raced in, swinging and dodging, performing moves that made my eyebrows hit my hairline.

Then it was Layne's turn with his new trident. He attacked another one of the snowmen, jabbing and spinning. His moves were fiercer than those he'd been practicing earlier in the living room in front of Cornelius.

I raised my gloved hand to my mouth. Something about the intensity on their faces told me this wasn't just play for them. They were small warriors, training for battle.

"They're sparring," Doc said, joining me.

"Where did they learn those moves?" That couldn't be innate, could it? Maybe with Addy, who was next in line to wear my shoes, but Layne? Only females could be Executioners.

"I've been training them."

I gaped at him. He was watching the two kids lunge and swing, destroying the snowmen. When had he trained my kids to … Oh! "Is this what you guys have been doing all of this time at the Rec Center?"

He nodded. "It started when Layne got suspended for defending your reputation at school. He wanted me to teach him how to fight. Instead, I taught him self-defense. Addy was eager to join us." He glanced my way. "Of course, like her mother, she's a natural with any sort of bat or other bludgeoning weapon."

I turned back to my daughter in time to see her slide on her knees under a snowman's twig arm, hop up on the backside of it, and land a blow to its middle section. "You've been teaching my kids how to defend themselves," I stated, as if cementing it in my head.

"I wanted to talk to you first and make sure you were okay with it, but the kids wanted to keep it a secret. They hoped to surprise you." I could feel his gaze on me. "I understand if you're upset about me not getting your permission first."

Layne landed a series of blows to his snowman's middle, and then spun around to add a kick that knocked off a twig arm. Addy shouted in approval, high-fiving her brother.

For months now I'd fretted about what would happen if any of my enemies came looking for my kids, picturing them as lambs to the slaughter. My heart swelled. The two warriors in front of me were not lambs. Sure, they were small, but maybe, just maybe, they could surprise an enemy enough to escape capture. Then I could hunt down whatever son of a bitch dared to come for my family and do what I was born to do.

I smiled at Doc. A real smile this time, not one of my think-positive faces. "You have given my kids the tools to stay alive in a world full of monsters. How could I be upset about a gift like that?"

"Mom!" Addy called, running toward me.

I leaned closer to Doc. "I'm going to rock your world tonight, Candy Cane."

His smile matched mine. "I have a sprig of mistletoe with your name on it."

Addy reached us, her cheeks pink, her grin broad. "How long have you been standing here?"

I pulled her in for a quick hug. "Long enough to see you and your brother kicking some serious snowman butt." Taking her hand, I led her over to Layne, who was breathing heavy, steam rising in puffs from his mouth. "You are both amazing! Where did you learn all of these killer moves?"

"Doc taught us," Layne said.

"We wanted to surprise you with what we've learned," Addy added.

"Trust me, I'm completely flabber-boozled." I picked up one of my favorite fast-pitch bats from my softball days, hefting it back and forth in my hands. The length and balance were made for increased swing speed and improved control. I'd hit more home runs than I could remember with this puppy. "How about it, you two? Feel like taking on your ol' ma to save the kingdom from doom?"

"Okay!" Addy grabbed her bat. "But you need to be ready for us, because Doc's a good teacher."

"We'll try to take it easy on you." Layne raised his trident, taking a defensive position.

I gripped the bat. "Bring it, buddy."

By the time we had tired from all of the swinging and dodging and laughing, I'd been slain multiple times by each of my kids. I was lying in the snow after yet another "deathblow" by Layne's trident when my mom yelled from the front porch that she had hot cocoa waiting.

Doc came over to help me up as the kids raced around to the front of the house. He brushed the snow off of me. "You fought bravely, but your children showed no mercy."

I laughed. "You trained them well."

He grabbed my bat from the snow at my feet. "They're naturals. After having seen you in action multiple times, I'm not surprised."

I stepped closer, lifting my face to his. "You interested in seeing me in action, too?"

He bent lower, his lips hovering over mine. "Always."

"Good." I went up on my toes, meeting his lips. At the same time, I slid a handful of snow under his coat and shirt.

His eyes widened as the ice hit his skin, his stomach tightening as he gasped. Before he could pull away, I shoved him backward, catching the back of his ankle with my toe. He fell flat on his back in the snow.

Leaning over him, I teased, "How do you like that action, big boy?"

He sat upright. "You'll pay for that, Vixen."

His hand shot out toward my leg, but I dodged out of

reach. Scrambling to his feet, he chased after me as I zigzagged through the snow.

I'd made it to the front porch by the time he caught me and lifted me over his shoulder. I squealed and struggled as he carried me to the yard where he plopped me down on my back and straddled my hips.

He scooped up a handful of snow. "Now, where should I put this?"

"Don't do it, *mon amour*," I said between giggles. "You love me, remember?"

"Don't even try that Morticia Addams trick with me. She loved pain."

Shoot. That was true. "How about we make a deal?"

"You've wheeled and dealed enough today, sweetheart."

I'd told Doc the whole ugly story of what had happened in Susan's room after I returned topside. He wasn't thrilled about my agreement to help her snag Rex if she untangled me from the Hooch mess, wondering how that would play out with the kids in the future. Truth be told, I seriously doubted Susan would fix the mess she'd made, so the Rex deal was most likely a moot point.

"What if I offer to give you my body tonight?" I asked.

"I was going to take it anyway."

I laughed. "Cocky. Nice. I like that."

"Yes, you will." He grabbed the bottom of my shirt. "Now, about this snow."

I opened my mouth to beg him not to do it, but before I could get a word out, Natalie came flying in from the side. She tackled Doc, driving him into the snow.

"Grab some snow, Vi!" she shouted, trying to hold him down with Addy's assistance.

"Pile up!" Addy yelled and threw herself on top of Doc's chest. The three of us pinned him long enough to stuff a couple more handfuls of snow under his shirt before my dad came out and threatened to help Doc if we didn't stop.

"You're lucky my dad came to your rescue," I teased Doc, helping him to his feet.

He shook out his shirt, laughing under his breath still. He leaned down and gave me a quick kiss. "You're right. I'm very lucky."

We headed inside to find all sorts of treats waiting for us in the kitchen, including hot buttered rum along with the cocoa.

After my hands and nose finally warmed up, I heard the sound of "Jingle Bells" coming from the living room.

"Is that a harmonica?" I asked my mom, who'd just breezed into the room with a pile of empty plates.

"Yes. Your friend Cornelius agreed to play some Christmas songs on it for the kids. He told Layne it belonged to his grandmother." She set the plates next to the sink. "He explained that she used the harmonica to soothe the spirits when they were feeling particularly ornery." She started back toward the living room but then stopped and aimed a frown in my direction. "That man is an odd duck, Violet."

Yeah, he was. I smiled. But so was I.

I left Doc and the others in the kitchen sipping their rum and followed Mom into the living room, joining my kids, Natalie, and Harvey. The kids and mom sang along to Cornelius's harmonica, with Harvey crooning in now and then, while Natalie and I watched and laughed.

Hours later, after it grew dark outside, Reid offered to take the kids out in the snowcat to see the neighborhood Christmas lights. They jumped up and down at the opportunity. Aunt Zoe, Mom, Dad, and Harvey went along with them, which left Doc, Cooper, Natalie, Cornelius, and me to hang out in front of the Christmas tree.

And that's when my goofy grin fell on Cooper.

I looked over at the soft, glowing lights of the tree

again, my heart feeling fat and sappy. For the moment, besides Susan's surprise Christmas gift of a dead husband, life was good. My coffer overflowed with the wealth of friendship, family, and love.

My focus returned to the puzzle, finding a piece of the fireplace that Cooper was putting together. I held it out across the card table. "You need this, Cooper."

He took it, stared at it, and fit it into place with a grunt.

"You're welcome, law dog."

"You two working on that puzzle together is so sweet," Natalie teased from where she was sprawled out on the loveseat. "Look at them, Doc. If I didn't know better, I'd say they actually liked each other."

Doc looked up from a book on World War II weapons that he'd borrowed from my dad's man-cave library. "Neither of them are biting each other at the moment. Must be the alcohol keeping their snarling at bay. What do you think, Cornelius? You're on the front line over there."

Cornelius was helping put the puzzle together from an upside-down view. When I'd offered to turn the table around, he'd told me that his third-eye chakra saw more clearly when items were rotated 180 degrees.

He held up a puzzle piece with Santa's red velvet suit, turning it this way and that in his fingers. "Two equally assertive members of a pack will find themselves in constant conflict unless they can develop mutual trust." He fit the piece into the puzzle. "I'd theorize that the detective and the Executioner have bonded over a common goal."

"You're wrong, Dr. Frankenstein," Cooper said. "My goal is to catch the bad guys. Parker's is to kill them." He tossed a piece of a stocking onto my side of the table. When I glanced up at him, he pointed out where it should go.

"I can see where it belongs, Cooper." I fit the piece in place. "Puzzle solving is one of my specialties. It's why I'm so good at solving *your* cases for you."

Natalie laughed. "Ka-pow! My girl isn't pulling her punches tonight."

I met Cooper's steely glare with a grin. "I'm kidding, *Coop*. We all know that you're an amazing detective with skills that would make Sherlock Holmes green with envy."

"Shut up and do the puzzle, Parker."

"Hey! You didn't correct me on your name."

A small grin played at the corner of his lips. "I know. Merry Christmas. That's your gift from me. Tomorrow, it's back to 'Cooper' or I'll shoot you."

Chuckling, I stood and stretched. "I love you, too, law dog. Anyone want a refill?" I held up my empty glass. Aunt Zoe's famous whiskey slush was starting to make my limbs feel nice and loose. "Coop?" I asked, using my present.

At his stiff nod, I grabbed his glass. Doc and Cornelius declined, still nursing theirs.

Natalie followed me to the kitchen. "Do you really think Susan will deliver on her promise to fix her mess?" She pulled the tub of whiskey slush from the freezer.

I'd filled in Natalie, too, about Susan's story. "I'd like to, but she doesn't have the best track record." I joined her at the counter, pointing at her nearly empty glass. "You need any more of that?"

"No. I've found my happy place for the moment and am going to sip this and then chill here for a while."

My happy place was back up in Deadwood with Doc and my kids by my side. It was fun being with my family all afternoon and evening, but I'd grown to love the sights and sounds and smells of Deadwood, snow or not.

At the moment, I didn't even mind all of the problems waiting for me up there, but that was probably the whiskey slush talking. I scooped a dollop of slush to keep my problems fenced in the background for a little longer.

I leaned closer to Natalie, shooting a glance at the doorway leading back to the living room. In a low voice, I said, "I double dog dare you to kiss Cooper under the mistletoe tonight."

She reached out and flicked my forehead.

"Owww!" I pulled back. "What'd you do that for?"

"Because you're being a drunken dipshidiot."

"I'm not drunk." I added another scoop of slush into my glass. "Just feeling more relaxed than usual."

"You deserve it tonight after the day you've had, what with getting married and losing your husband so quickly. I can feel your grief."

I scoffed. "That's the fastest I've ever gone through a man in my history of dating."

"Your soiled history."

"Like your history is any more clean and sparkly than mine."

"Isn't that the truth?" She frowned toward the living room. "Yet another reason I need to keep my hands to myself."

"You don't know how things will go with Cooper until you give him a try."

"If they don't go well, how's that going to affect our little group? It's awkward enough with me trying to hide that I'm hot for his bod. If I stoke that fire and then the flames go out later, we have a bigger problem than what we're dealing with now."

"So you're not even willing to try?"

She stared down into her glass. "I don't know."

"What are you going to do about the tension between you two?"

"I don't know."

"What *do* you know?"

She took a sip of her drink. "That I need to head south for a couple of weeks and put some distance between us."

"Distance makes the heart grow fonder."

"In this case, I want it to clear my brain so I can think

about the situation logically instead of getting sidetracked with naked thoughts about him." She blew out a breath. "Have you smelled him tonight? Maybe it's the whiskey talking, but I could eat him right up."

"It's the whiskey. He smells like Cooper plus cookies. And when have you ever thought logically about a guy?" I teased.

"I know, right?" She chuckled, but then sobered. "Seriously, ever since I went on this sabbatical from men, I've felt pretty damn good. No more insecurities, no more self-doubts, no more concerns about if what I'm doing or saying will cause a fight later. It's been really freeing."

"And lonely," I pointed out. I knew that from experience. I'd been on an involuntary sabbatical from men more often than not since having children.

She scowled. "And lonely."

I poured some lemon-lime soda pop over my whiskey slush. "I'm sure your cousins will be able to keep your mind off the bossy bonehead for a while."

"I talked to Claire earlier. Gramps wants her to help him tear down the General Store's rotting back deck and build a new one. She said she could use my help putting up with Gramps and his peanut gallery while we work."

I put away the whiskey slush and soda pop. "You always enjoy working with your hands."

"It's relaxing."

"What about the work you've been doing for Freesia at the old boarding house?"

"She's going to be in Nevada until after New Year's. Everything we've been doing is just for looks. There's nothing structural that needs my attention."

"I think you need to go then," I said.

"What about you?"

"What about me?"

"Are you going to be okay while I'm gone?"

"Probably not. I'm sure I'll pine for you hourly."

She laughed. "Besides pining, will you be able to keep your nose out of danger until I get back? I wouldn't want to miss out on any ghost hunts or monster parties."

"I'll do my best to wait for you before I run hell-bent into trouble again." I raised my glass toward her. "Here's to clearing your head."

She clinked her almost empty glass against mine. "With any luck, I'll be able to shake free of these sticky feelings and come back here a stronger and better woman."

"I'd settle for better looking," I joked, heading for the living room with drinks in hand.

She poked my ribs as I passed her, almost making me spill the drinks.

As I settled back into my chair in front of the puzzle, I glanced at Cooper. He was watching Natalie, who'd moved over by the window to stare out into the night. The longing on his face made my chest ache a little for him. If Natalie succeeded in her goal of conquering her libido, then he was going to be grouchier than a pissed-off wolverine for a long time to come. Maybe somebody should whisper in his ear about where she was going and why.

No, I needed to keep out of this, no matter how tempting it was to play cupid.

The front door opened and shut. I waited, expecting to hear my kids' voices.

"Is there any cherry pie left?" a familiar, deep voice called out.

I jumped out of my chair. "Quint!"

Natalie whirled from the window, a grin plastered on her face. "He made it!"

We raced to the foyer, both of us tackling my brother as he shrugged off his canvas winter coat.

After we gave him a moment to breathe, he looked around. His dark hair was a little longer than usual, curling around his collar, but his hazel eyes were bright and full of laughter and love, same as always. "Where is everyone?"

I told him, ending with Susan heading to Denver.

"Why Denver?"

Natalie and I frowned at each other.

"It's a long story," she said.

I pulled Quint toward the living room. "I'll explain it later. Come say hello to everyone else. I don't think you've met Cornelius."

A half hour later, the snowcat had returned and my mom and Aunt Zoe were spoiling my brother with hugs and cherry pie in the kitchen. Reid had taken my place at the puzzle table while Dad, the kids, and Natalie watched John Candy play the lovable *Uncle Buck* on the television. They'd finally burned out on Christmas shows.

Doc closed his book and wiggled his finger at me to come hither, leading the way to my old bedroom. He closed the door behind me. "Reid and Coop need to head back to Deadwood in the morning. They're taking the snowcat."

I nodded. "I wondered how long they could stay away before being called back to duty."

"I'm thinking about going with them so we can get your Honda off the side of the road. I can follow Reid's plow down Strawberry Hill."

"What about the snowstorm?" The flakes had stopped falling down in Rapid City, but that didn't mean the storm wasn't still dumping in the hills.

"It's stopped up there, too. Coop checked in with the facilities crew. They've been plowing through the holiday to clear the main roads. Strawberry and most of US 385 should be in pretty good shape by morning."

"Those poor guys didn't even get to enjoy Christmas."

"Coop said they were offered triple pay for their time."

"Oh, good." Extra money at Christmas always helped to cover the credit card bills that rolled in come January.

"Do you want to stay down here with your parents for another day or come back to Deadwood with us?"

"Let me talk to the kids and Aunt Zoe, see what they want to do."

"Don't forget about Elvis."

"Ha! That chicken stays with Addy. I'm off chicken duty for now." I sat down on the bed. "I think Natalie will want to go with you guys. She told me today she's heading down to Arizona as soon as she can get home and packed."

"Arizona, huh? Is she running to or from something?"

"From."

Doc nodded, catching my drift. "That's going to burn."

"I know. I'm tempted to say something to him."

"Violet, do you really—"

"But I won't," I cut in before he could warn me to mind my own business. I crossed my fingers behind my back, though, in case I had a change of heart.

"Cornelius wants to head back with us," Doc said. "He's anxious to check his video recordings to see what Jane's ghost has been up to while he was gone."

Of course he was. "What about Harvey?"

"He's in limbo. Your mom asked him to teach her how to cook Yorkshire pudding and a couple of his other dishes she'd heard about from your aunt."

"You think Aunt Zoe will be happy or sad that Reid is leaving?"

"They seem to be getting along at the moment."

"Yeah, but she keeps watching him with narrowed eyes when he's not looking. I'm not sure if that's good or bad."

"Me either. You Parker women don't make it easy on a poor guy."

"Give me a break. I roll over and show you my belly at a mere eyebrow wiggle."

"And a sexy belly it is." Doc came over and sat down next to me. "There's one other thing I need to talk to you about before we head back out with everyone else."

"What?"

He took my hand and dropped something in my palm. I looked down and laughed. "What am I supposed to do with this?" I held up the mistletoe that he'd plucked from Susan's decapitated snowman.

"I believe the instruction manual said something about holding it over your head and puckering your lips."

"Are you sure I'm not supposed to stick it down the front of my pants again?"

His grin was positively wicked. "We'll try that later." He took my hand with the mistletoe and lifted it high between us. "For now, give me those lips, Boots."

I licked them, closed my eyes, and waited for my last Christmas present of the day.

Doc delivered it and then some.

Chapter Nineteen

December 27th
Two days later on the road back to Deadwood …

I'd stayed an extra day at my parents' place, enjoying some time with my brother. Quint had hung around with us the day after Christmas until he'd had to catch a return flight back to the great white north to wrap up his photojournalist gig up there. Truth be told we were plenty white in South Dakota still, even though the sun had come out in full force and begun the long slow melt.

Aunt Zoe and Harvey had headed for Deadwood in her pickup last evening after Quint had taken off, leaving the kids and me to enjoy some alone time with my parents. The Twister game came out after supper. It turned out my mom's yoga exercises were good for more than relaxation and sex.

This morning, Doc had driven down in my SUV and picked me up. I had to meet with my out-of-town clients again later this afternoon and show them some more houses, which meant vacation was over.

After saying our good-byes to my kids and parents, we climbed into my SUV and headed into the hills the same way we'd come down in the snowcat. I wanted to see how much snow had piled up between Deadwood and Rapid City, so he was driving.

"How long are the kids staying?" he asked as we passed the trail to Buzzard's Roost on our way up into the hills on Highway 44.

"Dad will bring them home on New Year's Eve. He and

Mom have a party to go to that night that's for adults only."

We drove for a mile or two without talking. The snow grew deeper on the side of the road as we climbed. The radio started playing the Rolling Stones' hit "Wild Horses," as the DJ counted down to New Year's Day with what the station considered to be the top five hundred rock songs of all time. I leaned back in my warm seat, enjoying the gorgeous scenery alongside Doc, whose spicy cologne made my SUV smell wonderful.

"How was your brother?" Doc broke the silence.

"He was good. Although he seemed distracted. When I badgered him about what was going on, he asked me what I remembered about Dr. Hughes disappearing."

"Who's Dr. Hughes?"

"The father of Quint's best friend since childhood, Jeff Hughes."

"What do you remember?"

The road sign for Norris Peak Road had snow piled up around the post from the plows. It must have been almost four feet high.

"Not much," I told him. "Just that Dr. Hughes was an archaeologist, and that he went on a dig down in Mexico and never came back."

"Did you ask him why he was wondering about Dr. Hughes?"

"Yeah. He said he might try to look into Dr. Hughes' disappearance while he's down in Mexico on his next job." I shielded my eyes as the road turned and a ray of sun ricocheted off the snow, blinding me for a couple of seconds. "It kind of makes me nervous for him."

"Why's that?" Doc extended the visor to block the sun.

"I don't know. The Mexican jungle is not the safest place to go digging for dirt on a missing person."

"Maybe so, but the Black Hills have turned out to be a bit troublesome, too."

I snickered. "That's how the cow ate the cabbage."

He glanced my way. "You've been hanging around Harvey too much."

"I can't help it. He lures me in with his cooking and then fills my head with his sayings."

Several minutes of listening and driving later, Doc slowed as we approached US Highway 385. "Did you get a chance to tell Quint about being an Executioner?"

"No. Between the kids, my parents, and Aunt Zoe wanting time with him, we weren't alone much." And when we were, the time never seemed right.

He turned, heading for Deadwood. "You're dragging your feet."

"Maybe."

"Why?"

I shrugged. "I'm not sure where to start with this whole Executioner business." I scowled out the window at the snow-coated pine trees. "And part of me doesn't want him to know I'm a killer."

"You think that will bother him?"

"He's never been much for violence. An offshoot of our flower-child mother's philosophy, I suppose." Where had I gone awry? Was it because I was born to kill?

Pink Floyd's "Comfortably Numb" came through the speakers as the radio counted down to the next song. I turned the song up. "Whoever came up with this top five hundred list doesn't know shit. This song should be much higher on the chart. Or lower. You know what I mean."

Doc turned the volume down. "I agree, but you're avoiding my question, sweetheart."

I sighed. "What if Quint starts looking at me differently?"

Susan had been right about one thing. I adored my brother. I always had. Next to Natalie, he was my best friend growing up. How was I supposed to tell him what I was up to these days without coming across as stark raving mad? Or at least slightly unhinged? And if he did believe me, I didn't want him to look at me like I was a killer, even though I was. I preferred him thinking of me as his crazy but lovable "Curly Bill."

"Violet, you can't hide what you are forever. Trust me, I know from experience. You can pretend, but something always gives you away."

"I know, I know. I just didn't want to ruin the holiday."

"Your sister already beat you to it."

I shifted in my seat. "Boy howdy, she sure did a bang-up job of it this year."

"Have you heard from her?"

"No. Mom texted her but got no reply."

"You think she made it to St. Barts?"

"Maybe. But it's very possible she fled to South America instead, leaving me in a lurch with a bunch of money that doesn't belong to me."

Doc's mouth tightened. "Coop thinks you should hire a lawyer."

"Dad is going to contact his this week. He told me that my mom insists on paying for whatever it takes to fix this."

The snow had turned Pilot Knob's craggy top into a white blob. I'd bet Custer Peak was the same if not more buried.

"How's your dad doing with this Susan business? He was pretty quiet at the table when it all came out."

"We had a one-on-one conversation in his man cave after you guys left. He told me that after Susan had spoken her piece at the dinner table and Mom had calmed down, she and Dad had followed Susan to the basement. My mother spelled it out clearly without mincing words that Susan needed to do right by me. Dad added that my sister was not allowed back in their house until the deed was done."

"No wonder Susan went to Denver with Mr. Peabody."

"Dad said she went way too far this time, even for my mother's forgiving nature."

"Did you tell him about your deal with her for Rex?"

"No way. That would only piss him off at me. Besides, the chances of Susan following through on her word are slim at best. She has a history of taking the easy road out of trouble town." The sign to Roubaix Lake was half-coated with snow with a drift burying the posts. "I'll deal with Rex if I need to when the time comes." I glanced at Doc. "Unless I kill him first."

"You'll need to get in line behind Natalie. She told me she has a brand-new pink hammer with his name on it."

I grinned. "She called me last night from the Wyoming–Colorado border."

Natalie hadn't dallied up in Deadwood. She'd ridden back to town with Doc and Cornelius, packed her bags, and left a couple of hours later. "She should be pulling into Jackrabbit Junction later this evening if the roads are clear the rest of the way south."

"That's a long drive in a short time."

"She was pretty determined to put distance between her and a certain detective." I held my hand up in front of the warm air coming from the dashboard vents, glad for the heat with all of the snow surrounding us. "Does Cooper know she's gone?"

Doc nodded. "I mentioned it this morning before I left for Rapid. He was heading to work as I drove away."

"Did you tell him why she went down there?"

A smile played at the corner of his lips. "I might have hinted at it."

I doubted Doc hinted as hard as I would have, but the cupid in me was content for now. "How'd he take it?"

"Hard to tell with Coop. He wears that same expression for most everything."

"If you mean the pissed-off one, I wish he'd switch it out more often." A couple of snowmobilers passed us going the other way, cruising at the edge of the ditch. "He's actually a little handsome when he smiles, but not as dreamy as Reid."

A laugh came from Doc's side of the cab. "I'll be sure to let Coop know you said that next time he smiles at me."

"Oh, Lord, please don't. He'll shoot me for sure."

He caught my hand and squeezed it. "Are you ready to return to life in Deadwood?"

"Life and death and everything in between." I laced my fingers with his. "Anything happen while I was gone?"

He grimaced in response.

"What?" When he still held his tongue, I leaned toward him. "Come on, Doc. Spill."

"I wanted to give you time to get home and unpack before telling you."

"Telling me what?" His reluctance to talk made my chest flutter.

He frowned out the windshield. "As I promised Addy, I stopped by your aunt's place shortly after getting back to Deadwood yesterday morning to check on the cat and gerbil."

"Please tell me they're both alive."

"They're fine."

Whew! The last thing I needed right now was a dead pet to deal with on top of a dead husband.

"But when I was in our room," Doc continued. "I looked out the window and saw someone standing on the sidewalk in front of the house."

"Was it Rex?"

He shook his head. "Dominick Masterson."

"Damn it." I pulled my hand free of his and crossed my arms. "That man is relentless. You didn't talk to him, did you?"

Dominick had a way of getting into people's heads. Only Harvey and I had been able to resist his so-called charm to date: Me because of what I was, and Harvey because … well, we didn't know why, only that he could. Cooper's theory was that his uncle's head was too hard for anything to get inside of it, let alone stick.

"I intended to see what he wanted, but by the time I made it downstairs and opened the front door, he was gone. I walked around the outside of the house twice, but saw no sign of him other than tracks in the snow, which led up the hillside to Mount Moriah."

"Crap." I blew out a breath. "You know what this means, right? Dominick is out of patience and I have to hunt down his stupid *lidérc* sooner rather than later."

"No, *we* have to hunt down his *lidérc*." He looked my way for a second before returning his focus on the snow-covered road. "We're a team, remember?"

"I have a feeling this is going to get really hairy fast."

"Great." He spared me a grin. "That's exactly how I like my women—hairy and fast."

I chuckled, watching the trees go by out the window. Pink Floyd faded, replaced by AC/DC's hard-core riffs.

"Okay, it's official. This song list is total hogwash. 'Back in Black' is always in the top one hundred if not top fifty. I've lost all faith in this radio station."

Doc hit a button and the stereo went dark. The crunch of tires on snow filled the cab. "What's really bothering you, Violet?"

Dominick Masterson's handsome face flickered through my thoughts, making me grit my teeth. That asshole needed to stay away from Aunt Zoe. "Where's that damned *lidérc* hiding?"

Doc's brow furrowed. "A more worrisome question is how in the hell are we going to catch a parasitic, soul-sucking Hungarian devil?"

"I have an idea about that." An old co-worker in the Executioner business had given me a tip on hunting *lidérc* a short time ago.

"Oh, yeah? Let's hear it."

"For starters, we're going to need some fresh bait." I grimaced out the window at the picturesque winter scene. "As in the non-human kind."

The End … for now

A quick note from Ann:

If you'd like to read about Quint's adventures down in Mexico while searching for Dr. Hughes at the last Maya dig site where the archaeologist was seen, check out *Look What The Wind Blew In*, the first book in my ongoing Dig Site Mystery Series.

Also, be sure to catch up with Natalie's cousins, the Morgan sisters, down in Arizona in my Jackrabbit Junction Mystery Series. Word on the street is that more crazy high jinks are coming soon from their neck of the Sonoran Desert. With Natalie heading their way, you're not going to want to miss what happens next at the Dancing Winnebago R.V. Park!

AUNT ZOE'S WHISKEY SLUSH RECIPE

Ingredients:
Water — 4¼ cup
Sugar — ½ cup
Frozen lemonade — 6 ounces
Frozen orange juice — 6 ounces
Whiskey — 1½ cups

Instructions:

— Heat 3¼ cups of water to boiling and then add ½ cups of sugar. Stir until sugar is dissolved.

— Add frozen lemonade and frozen orange juice.

— Add 1 cup of cool water.

— Mix in 1½ cups of whiskey.

— Freeze until slushy.

Party time:

— Fill a glass half full of whiskey slush.

— Add 7-UP.

Enjoy!

About the Author

Ann Charles is a USA Today bestselling author who writes award-winning mysteries that are splashed with humor, adventure, romance, paranormal, and whatever else she feels like throwing into the mix. When she is not dabbling in fiction, arm-wrestling with her children, attempting to seduce her husband, or arguing with her sassy cats, she is daydreaming of lounging poolside at a fancy resort with a shot of tequila in one hand and a great book in the other.

Facebook (Personal Page):
http://www.facebook.com/ann.charles.author

Facebook (Author Page):
http://www.facebook.com/pages/Ann-Charles/37302789804?ref=share

Twitter (as Ann W. Charles):
http://twitter.com/AnnWCharles

Ann Charles Website:
http://www.anncharles.com

More Books by Ann

Books in the Deadwood Mystery Series

WINNER of the 2010 Daphne du Maurier Award for Excellence in Mystery/Suspense

WINNER of the 2011 Romance Writers of America® Golden Heart Award for Best Novel with Strong Romantic Elements

Welcome to Deadwood—the Ann Charles version. The world I have created is a blend of present day and past, of fiction and non-fiction. What's real and what isn't is for you to determine as the series develops, the characters evolve, and I write the stories line by line. I will tell you one thing about the series—it's going to run on for quite a while, and Violet Parker will have to hang on and persevere through the crazy adventures I have planned for her. Poor, poor Violet. It's a good thing she has a lot of gumption to keep her going!

Short Stories from Ann's
Deadwood Mystery Series

The Deadwood Shorts collection includes short stories featuring the characters of the Deadwood Mystery series. Each tale not only explains more of Violet's history, but also gives a little history of the other characters you know and love from the series. Rather than filling the main novels in the series with these short side stories, I've put them into a growing Deadwood Shorts collection for more reading fun.

The Jackrabbit Junction Mystery Series

Bestseller in Women Sleuth Mystery and Romantic Suspense

Welcome to the Dancing Winnebagos R.V. Park. Down here in Jackrabbit Junction, Arizona, Claire Morgan and her rabble-rousing sisters are really good at getting into trouble—BIG trouble (the land your butt in jail kind of trouble). This rowdy, laugh-aloud mystery series is packed with action, suspense, adventure, and relationship snafus. Full of colorful characters and twisted up plots, the stories of the Morgan sisters will keep you wondering what kind of a screwball mess they are going to land in next.

The Dig Site Mystery Series

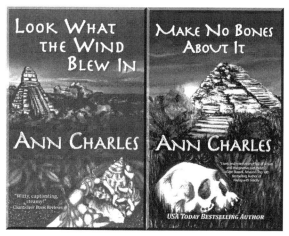

Welcome to the jungle—the steamy Maya jungle that is, filled with ancient ruins, deadly secrets, and quirky characters. Quint Parker, renowned photojournalist (and lousy amateur detective), is in for a whirlwind of adventure and suspense as he and archaeologist Dr. Angélica García get tangled up in mysteries from the past and present in exotic dig sites. Loaded with action and laughs, along with all sorts of steamy heat, these books will keep you sweating along with the characters as they do their best to make it out of the jungle alive.

The AC Silly Circus Mystery Series

"My life was one, big, fun freakshow until someone killed my favorite clown. Now, not even watching a grizzly bear eat a flaming torch made me crack a smile."
~Madam Electra~

From the AC Silly Circus Co. comes a new series of paranormal mystery novellas chock-full of oddball shapeshifters, dangerous secrets, spicy steam, and loads of laughs.

Step right up and enjoy the freakshow!

The Goldwash Mystery Series

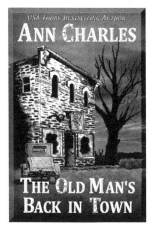

A sizzling, suspenseful SHORT STORY wrapped in a puzzling mystery that will leave you hungry for more.

It's "Groundhog Day" meets the modern day Old West!

In the lonely mining ghost town of Goldwash, Nevada, Christmas has come early. Unfortunately, the local bar owner must be on this year's naughty list, because Santa brought her something even worse than a piece of coal on this dark, cold winter night—her old man.

Made in the USA
Columbia, SC
26 November 2018